Justine Orme

ARABELLA –

BY THE SWORD OF THE LORD
AND THE WORD OF HER TESTIMONY

Text copyright © 2021 by Justine Orme

All rights reserved.
First Published 2021

Justine Orme reserves the moral right to be identified as the author of this work.

Short extracts, prayers, worship stanzas, and brief quotations, may be copied for non-profit personal use only without prior permission.

Otherwise, no part of this publication may be reproduced, stored in a retrieval system, or transmitted in any form or by any means, electronic, mechanical, photocopying, scanning or otherwise, without the prior written consent of the author.

Cover Art: Arabella, © Rosemary Williamson
https://www.facebook.com/Rosemary-Williamson-Art-1522275818052587
Cover Design and other interior artwork: Jan Kaluza

Editor & Co-Publisher: Colleen Kaluza of
WordWyze Publishing, New Zealand – HTTP://WordWyze.nz

Photos of Justine Orme: © 2018 Colleen Kaluza

Printed in New Zealand by YourBooks.co.nz
Available from IngramSpark and Amazon POD providers
A catalogue record for this book is available from the National Library of New Zealand

Printed Soft-cover Edition: ISBN-13: 978-0-473-60368-7
Epub Edition: ISBN-13: 978-0-473-60369-4

DEDICATION

I was sitting in my chair, doing nothing in particular, when the Lord said,

"Arabella."

"What about Arabella, Lord?" I asked Him.

He then downloaded the entire blueprint for this book.

As I approached the end of the writing process, following what Father showed me, I was astounded to have two baby girls born within six hours of each other, in different parts of the world, both named Arabella.

To all the Arabellas out there, called according to the purposes of God.

And to all the Evelyns who support and love the Arabellas.

And especially to the two little Arabellas who were born just as I finished writing this book.

May you fulfil the destiny that Father prophesied to you before you left His heart for this earth.

Arabella in Kenya

Born 7:00 pm 15 October 2021

(Kenya time – GMT+2)

(5am 16 October 2021, NZ time)

Manna-Arabella in India

Born 03:30 am

16 October 2021

(Indian Time – GMT+4.5)

(11am 16 October 2021,
NZ Time)

Photos provided by the families and published with permission.

BY THE SWORD OF THE LORD AND THE WORD OF HER TESTIMONY

ARABELLA

PROLOGUE

Father called "ארה בלה Ara-bella", and quietly, gently, put his hand to his heart, waiting for the response. It came, as the tiny, shimmering rainbow-clad spirit glided from heart to hand.

"Beloved," Father said, "Your time has come. Are you ready to go to the earth and do all I will write in your book of life?"

The scribe was waiting patiently before the Lord's throne, his finger poised to write all that God Almighty would decree and sing over this little one.

The diminutive spirit-being jumped up and down, the garment of shining iridescent colours reflecting the colour coming from her Father.

"I take that as a yes, then," He laughed.

Love illumined the spirit standing on Father's hand. And Love started to speak. The scribe began to write.

"The name your mother and father will give you on the earth will be Arabella. This name identifies who you are, your calling and your destiny. עארה Ara means lion, and so, you shall be as a lion roaring into the realms above the earth, shattering bondages and chains. בל Bell, for your striking against the enemy is as a hammer striking at an anvil, many, many, many, times. בלה Bella, for it means beautiful. And so, you are." The Father paused and looked at the Son. "And 'A' is the first letter of the Hebraic and the English and Greek alphabets. A is for אלף Aleph or Alpha. The first, the beginning. It is the first letter in my name of Adonai. Thus, you have my stamp of approval, my D.N.A. in your name."

The tiny spirit tinkled in joy and then hesitated, "Father, I love you, and I will do as you say, but will I ever see you again? You are life and love, and I cannot live without your love; I do not want to be without you."

Father God smiled. "Beloved Arabella, I will never leave you. I will never forsake you. And look, I have appointed Eliora to be with you throughout your life on earth, and when your purposes are fulfilled, you will return to us here, never to leave again." Father paused and looked at Arabella as though seeing right into her very heart. "Do you agree?"

Arabella stood very still, looking at her beloved Father's face. "Yes, Father. I agree."

God beckoned to the Angel Eliora and gently put Arabella into Eliora's hand.

Bowing before the Almighty, Eliora flew with Arabella through time and space, realms and worlds, to the dimension of Earth.

All heaven watched as the tiny explosion of brilliant light known as conception took place.

Eliora guarded the mother and child vigilantly.

◈◈

David was in his favourite place; the children's garden, where he was planting flowers. He was making a garden, which outlined a striped tiger with marigolds for the orange stripes and the darkest pansies for the black. He had chosen well, using lighter shades of each flower as the colours faded towards the tiger's belly. Real tigers prowled around, watching his progress and growling their advice. The children squealed in delight, hugging the tigers who licked the children in love. The flowers sang in joy. Some of the Nursery Angels stopped to watch, noting that the creativity in mankind was like that of the Lord God Himself.

"Such a magnificent creation," they murmured to each other. "Do you remember when the Lord first made man, so much in his likeness that he was as Elohim Himself?"

Looking up from his work, David noticed a man approaching. His smile widened as he recognised Jesus, who called out to him. "David. Come and spend some time with me. I have something to share with you."

Dropping his tools on the ground, David ran to Jesus. Nothing was better than to be with Him.

The tigers and children bounded past David,

leaping onto Jesus. They all sprawled in a mess on the ground, tigers, Jesus and children, a pandemonium of legs, arms, and tigers' tails amidst squeals of laughter and loud purring.

The messenger angel, Keziah, watched together with the nursery angels and laughed at the fabulousness of God as man, delighting in his family.

Jesus grinned at his friend David who was watching the melee in great amusement. Gently untangling himself from the children and cats, the Lord reached for David's hand, who hauled him to his feet. David felt the rough silvery scar, palm to palm.

As angels gathered up the children, Jesus and the man walked off together. Throwing his arm over David's shoulder, he said: "Come with me."

Keziah followed them.

David would have been an old man before reaching their destination if their journey had been in earth-time, for all they came across wanted to touch Jesus, be held by him, love him and all burst into glorious worship. No one was turned away. Jesus led David through the wide paved avenues of pure, translucent gold. There was nothing like this on earth, nothing to which it compared. The avenues were lined with fruit trees. These trees had fascinated David when he had arrived home, for each tree bore many different types of fruit, and curiously when eating the fruit, though the juice dripped onto his hand, his hands were not sticky afterwards. There was no decay in Heaven. All was clean and fresh and bright; brighter, crisper colours than he had ever experienced on earth.

After the many interruptions, they arrived at their destination, the viewing room. Settling before the expanse known as the heavens, Jesus indicated that David should sit. "Watch", He said, as He opened the veil between Heaven and the earth.

More angels came in. Keziah stood behind David.

They all watched as Jesus pulled two realms together. Heaven touching earth. Through the spoken word, and with His own hands, Jesus reached into eternity, stretched through time, grasping eternity in one hand and time in the other, pulling them together, so they were enmeshed as one. His glory emitted the purest light that enveloped all.

David sat back, entranced. It was not a new experience, but it wasn't often given to him. The Lord traversed between times and dimensions, realms and kingdoms regularly, and just sometimes, David had been allowed a glimpse, such as the time when his granddaughter had been born.

The focus zoomed through eternity into time, and David was startled to see his earth home and his wife. "Evie, oh my Evie," He leaned forward. She was as beautiful as ever he had seen her.

"Watch now, my friend. Take joy in what you see." Jesus turned to David and smiled at him.

Resplendence quivered through the atmosphere.

CHAPTER ONE

"Do you have the advert ready?" Keziah asked Achim, the scribe angel.

Achim's office looked as though a whirlwind of angels had stormed through it, throwing a party on their way. There were scrolls upended onto the floor, and crumpled up scrolls tossed vaguely in the direction of an already overflowing bin. His assistant Habib was calmly sorting out the scroll rack. Keziah smiled to herself. Achim was well known for his eccentricity when he was creating. She peered over his shoulder at what he was working on.

She read:

> WE NEED MORE THAN A NANNY
> WE WANT TO ADOPT A GRANNY
> Arabella needs a Grandma.
> As two busy professional parents,
> we are looking for someone to look after
> our beautiful 12-year-old daughter
> That one special person will live in.

> We want you to be part of our family,
> To be a part of our lives, doing all those wonderful grandmother things.
> You will have your own cottage on our property.
> You MUST love Jesus and have similar life perspective and goals.
> A clean driver's licence
> and your own car are essential.
> The Grandma days and times will be discussed over our first cup of coffee, as will salary.
> Contact us to talk.

"That's good," Keziah enthused, "Holy Spirit has been working in Evelyn's heart, and the Three in One are ready to proceed. Evelyn's angels have been gently helping her move forward. Now, the framework is in place; it's time for the next phase."

Habib looked at Keziah from where he was gathering up the scrolls off the floor and smiled. "He'll have it finished in time."

CHAPTER TWO

"Lord, it's been so long since David went to live with you, and I'm lonely." Evelyn wiped the tears off her cheeks. "Yes, I know you will never leave me, but Father, I'm worried about money. David left death insurance, but what we thought was a huge amount all those years ago, is absolutely nothing now. I can't stay in our home any longer; I can't afford it. I know there's no mortgage to pay, but the taxes, the maintenance; David used to do all this. I can't do it." A little sob hiccupped its way up, with others threatening a dam burst.

Evelyn reached for the ever-present box of tissues to blow her nose and wipe the tears, precious tears, off her face.

Unseen in the earth realm, Janel collected the tears that had spilt over Evelyn's cheeks, catching them in a crystal vial. As she did so, they were immediately transferred to the Room of Remembrance in Heaven.

Evelyn wandered around the house she and David had bought when they were first married, over forty years ago now. It was so quiet, but every room was alive with memories: the children laughing, fighting among themselves, their music echoing in her mind. She proceeded upstairs to their bedroom with its whispers of their intimacy. Times of grief were shared in this room. Times of joy and love. Just life. All their lives together centred in this room, including times of anger, slammed doors and cold responses. She smiled ruefully at how childish it all seemed now. Scenes ran rapidly through her memory and heart.

Janel followed her through the silent house.

Walking down the hallway, the photos on the walls seemed to smile at her. Her *rogues' gallery*, she called it—the place where David had hung their now faded wedding photo. Over the years, family portraits had followed: the children as newborns, birthdays, celebrations, graduations and then their wedding photos and the photos of the grandchildren; her parents, and David's parents, long gone now. She paused at their wedding photo. "So young. We were so young," she whispered, running a finger down the picture of her husband, tracing the much-loved face, now gone. Her eyes moved along the wall of images, stopping at the one of her youngest son, Christopher. She gave a small laugh at this picture. Her son, the only ginger-haired, freckle-faced boy in a group of dark-skinned, dark-haired boys. A very Scottish looking child in amongst his Māori school friends at their Kapa Haka class. "You were so funny, so determined to see past skin colour. And you succeeded." She was very proud of him. Her eyes moved to the last photo David had hung on the wall just before he died, their ruby wedding anniversary. Grief rose again. "I miss you so much, David. Lord, why?" she wailed.

'If only you could see,' Janel whispered, *'All those people are not gone. They are no longer in this realm, but they are still alive.'*

All three of Evelyn and David's children had called her over and over. *Mum. Come and live near us. Sell that big house. You'll be near the grandchildren.* But somehow, she couldn't. Maybe it was because being in their home kept David's memory closer, or perhaps it was fear of the unknown. She fought back the panic when she even thought about the enormous task of selling up, clearing out all the furniture—settling into a new town, making new friends. Her long-time friend Michelle had also encouraged her. "Go, go on," she'd said. And to prove that moving away wasn't an issue at any age, Michelle had moved to another country: Ireland.

"Give me wisdom, Lord," Evelyn cried. "Should I sell and go and live near one of the children?" Talking to God as her friend wasn't strange to Evelyn. It was her life. He was so close to her. Sometimes she felt as though she could feel Papa

God holding her close. "Right," she said out loud. "Get a grip, Evie. Time to put on your big girl panties and take the world on again. Enough of this self-pity."

In the other realm, Wisdom heard Evelyn cry out to her and immediately came, bringing gifts, which she then placed onto Evelyn's future path, her gift of wisdom. Janel listened as Wisdom gave further instructions and left again.

Evelyn's days passed by, between coffee dates with friends and struggling to maintain the garden. *David's garden,* she thought, *How he had loved pottering in the garden.*

It was a bright Wednesday afternoon. Not quite Summer; very late Spring. There was so much to do. David would have had all the fruit trees sprayed, the weeding done, the summer garden planted and seeds sown for the next crop. Evie stayed on her knees, weeding. They were aching, her shoulders tense with frustration. "I can't do it all, Lord." She sat there in the middle of the vegetable garden and cried. "I have to sell, Father; I just can't manage this all alone. But it seems so disloyal to David and all he did."

Janel looked up as she sensed another angel's arrival. Zarad appeared, smiling at Janel. "It's time," he said. Janel clapped her hands in delight, and going over to Evelyn, nudged her, whispering, *'it's time to go inside and make a cup of tea.'*

Wearily, Evelyn got to her feet, stretching and massaging the small of her back, kneading out the aches from bending over. Leaving the gardening tools where they were, she went inside to the kitchen. *I'll have a cup of tea,* she thought, *and then go back outside to do some more.*

Sitting on the back porch with her steaming cup of tea in hand, she looked at all the work she still had to do. But as she looked, she saw not the work that had to be done but all she had achieved: the weeding, the planting, and a distinct feeling of satisfaction nestled in her heart.

"Evelyn, dearest beloved," the Master whispered to her. "I have something more. The winter season has passed. The rain has gone. It is time to live again." The Master's voice brought peace, soothing her pain.

CHAPTER THREE

"I'm really worried," Niccola said to Joshua. "What if we choose the wrong Grandmother? What if we let someone bad into our lives?" She fidgeted with her silver chain necklace. "What if we inadvertently bring something terrible into Bella's life?"

Both Niccola and Joshua's angels looked at each other and smiled. The Lord couldn't have given them a better assignment. These two just emanated love, their hearts resonating with the Father's.

Joshua looked at his wife. "Honey, we have prayed about this. We have been through everything. But above all, I trust Bella's instinct. She's very alert and onto it. She can see right through people."

"That's true. But I'm a mother. It's my job to worry!" Niccola ran away giggling as Joshua poked her in the ribs. "Put the barbecue on, Josh; we'll eat outside tonight," she called back over her shoulder.

Later, as the family gathered around the outdoor table, Niccola beamed a great smile of joy at her small family. "It's so nice for the three of us to be together. I wish we had more family time." The late evening sun gave its last warmth of the day, blending shadows with dancing light.

Niccola put her hand over Arabella's. "Bel, we need to talk about the Granny thing again. Dad and I have worked out the advert, and we've all talked about why we need someone more than just a nanny. You have had nannies before, but with my work becoming busier, we need someone on whom we can rely. Honey, we live so far away from your grandparents, and we really feel you need someone to be there for you, always. We work such long hours. It's not good that you are alone." She looked carefully at her daughter, gauging her reaction. "We've prayed about it together. Dad says to trust your instincts. So now, tell us what you think of the ad."

Joshua put a piece of paper in front of his twelve-year-old daughter. "Read it carefully, Bel."

The girl pulled the typed sheet of paper towards her and read aloud

WE NEED MORE THAN A NANNY
WE WANT TO ADOPT A GRANNY
Arabella needs a Grandma.
As two busy professional parents,
we are looking for someone to look after
our beautiful 12-year-old daughter.

That one special person will live in.
We want you to be part of our family,
To be a part of our lives,
doing all those wonderful grandmother things.
You will have your own cottage
on our property.
You MUST love Jesus and have similar life perspectives and goals.
A clean driver's licence and
your own car are essential.
The Grandma days and times will be discussed
over our first cup of coffee, as will salary
Contact us to talk.

Arabella looked up from reading the typed advert. "Why does her driver's licence have to be clean? Does she need to wash it? I've never seen you wash yours?"

Joshua roared with laughter. "Trust my girl," he said. "No, Honey. A clean driver's licence doesn't mean it has to be washed; it means that the person mustn't have any drink driving charges or a lot of speeding fines. That sort of thing."

"Oh! Ok then." Arabella read the ad again and finally looked up at her parents. "Yes. I want a grandma. Will she be able to do baking with me?"

Eliora giggled. She loved the child she had been assigned to. There was such light and fun in her.

"If you want her too," Niccola nodded at her daughter. "We are hoping that we will get someone who already has grandmother experience so that she can come already trained!"

"Mum! You don't train grandmothers! That is just weird."

This child was delightful. The Lord had created a beautiful piece of His heart. Eliora sighed contentedly.

CHAPTER FOUR

Evelyn was starting to relax. Finishing her tea, she replaced the cup on the saucer, admiring, as always, the beauty of the bone china. Her friends had started drinking their tea and coffee from bone china now. Somehow it made it all taste that much better than in a mug. Just as she stood up to take her cup back inside, she heard a knock at the front door.

"Now, who could that be? A visitor, how exciting!" she talked to herself as she put her cup and saucer on the kitchen counter and walked quickly down the hallway to open the front door, her steps echoing in the emptiness of the house.

Glancing quickly through the top glass panes of the door, Evie checked to see who the caller was. David had taught her to do that. *Safety Evie. Always check.* She looked. There was no one there. Carefully she opened the door leaving her foot pushed against the bottom of the door in case she had to shut it in a hurry, and peered out. The front veranda was empty, just the swing rocking gently in the breeze. She didn't see the angel on the porch swing. "Hello," she called, "Who is it?"

She couldn't see Zarad standing in front of her, his wings folded. Evie took a step forward, looking around to see who had knocked. *'Take another step outside,'* Zarad whispered.

She was perplexed. She had definitely heard the knock on the door. *Probably just some kids playing tricks*, she thought and stepped out onto the porch to check anyway, stopping abruptly as a rustling, crunching sound came from under her right foot.

Evie looked down. A newspaper? She bent down and picked the paper up, noticing an advert circled with a bright red marker pen,

**WE NEED MORE THAN A NANNY
WE WANT TO ADOPT A GRANNY**

What on earth? she thought. *Who would leave me a paper with an advert marked out?* Looking around again, still not seeing anyone, she went back inside, holding the newspaper and shutting the door behind her. Zarad followed her through the closed door, nodding to Janel. "All is going to plan," he said. Janel nodded, smiling at him. The two angels walked behind Evelyn as she went back to where she had been sitting on the back porch.

Evelyn was bewildered. Glancing at the advert that had the big red thick circle around it, she put the paper down on the old wicker table and went back into the kitchen, distractedly putting the kettle on, making another cup of tea.

Sipping her tea, she wandered back out to the porch and picked the paper up again, reading the ad:

WE NEED MORE THAN A NANNY
WE WANT TO ADOPT A GRANNY

Arabella needs a Grandma.
As two busy professional parents,
we are looking for someone to look after
our beautiful 12-year-old daughter.
That one special person will live in.
We want you to be part of our family,
To be a part of our lives,
doing all those wonderful grandmother things.
You will have your own cottage
on our property.
You MUST love Jesus and have similar life perspectives and goals.
A clean driver's licence and
your own car are essential.
The Grandma days and times will be discussed
over our first cup of coffee, as will salary.
Contact us to talk.

She turned the paper over to the other side, hoping to gain clues, but it was only the local paper; nothing out of the ordinary. Perplexed, she let the paper fall onto her lap and thoughtfully picked the cup up again.

"Lord, what is this about?" Evelyn spoke aloud, no one except the birds, bees and butterflies to hear her, and they didn't take the slightest notice. And the beloved unseen guest, Jesus himself, together with Janel and Zarad. If Evelyn could but look with the eyes of her heart, she would have seen Jesus sitting on the porch steps, looking at her.

"Read it carefully, beloved," Jesus said.

She put the cup down on the table, and picking the paper up again, read every line, every word, looking for clues, any hint of what she was to do with this most extraordinary newspaper advert. How had it arrived on her doorstep? Why would someone do that? Distractedly, she picked her cup up again.

Jesus smiled. "Excellent. Now, why don't you call Christina and Angela and ask them to come over for coffee? You could discuss this with them." He spoke to Evelyn's heart.

Zarad bowed to the Lord and disappeared.

CHAPTER FIVE

Angela sniffed at the aroma of fresh baking greeting her as she came around the back to find Evelyn. Friends didn't knock on the front door, the back door had always been open and welcoming when David had walked the earth, and just because he was gone, Evelyn saw absolutely no need to change the warmth of her hospitality.

Duriel, who accompanied Angela, waved a greeting to Janel. The two angels stood together, their eyes shining in delight.

"Evie, I came immediately. This is so intriguing," Angela hugged Evelyn whilst inhaling appreciatively as she eyed the cookies cooling on the rack. "How on earth did you have time to call us, then bake something, so it's ready when we get here?"

Smiling at her long-time friend, Evelyn laughed. "It's really easy. I'm a lazy cook, you know. If it's too time-consuming, I don't bother." Angela just looked at her sceptically. She couldn't cook anything and relied on her husband to feed them. "I couldn't possibly do all you do. Without Harry to cook for us, I would be forced to eat out. Or starve!" Her blues eyes lit up. "Oooh, now there's an idea. That's one way for me to lose weight!" she ran her hands down over her waist and hips.

"Honey," Evie grinned at her friend. "Who wants to cuddle a skinny bag of bones. Harry sure wouldn't." Angela's perceived weight issue was legendary.

"Can I smell chocolate cookies?" Christina bustled into the kitchen, hugging first Evelyn, then Angela. "Omigosh, Evie. You are amazing!" Christina snuck a cookie from the rack and popped it straight into her mouth, cheeks bulging, eyes round with mischief.

The three women laughed. Evie put the coffee on to brew, the enticing fragrance of the coffee mixing with the tantalising aroma of the cookies.

"Come on then, let's go outside," Evelyn loaded the tray with coffee, cups and cookies, and carried it out to the back porch, pouring three cups of coffee and handing them around.

"Bone china. There is *nothing* like it." Christina was appreciative of the finer things in life.

"Now then, Evie," Angela said, "What is this about?"

Evelyn picked up the paper and handed it to her. Christina read the ad over Angela's shoulder.

Angela carefully folded the paper and laid it on the table. There was complete silence. The three women sat staring at each other.

Janel giggled. Adira, who went everywhere with Christina, stood with her hands on Christina's shoulders and laughed aloud. Duriel, standing by Angela, had a big grin on his face. "If anyone can push through Evelyn's reserve, it will be Angela," he said.

"Well!" Christina broke the silence.

"Well," Angela looked thoughtful. "Where do you suppose the paper came from? How could it suddenly just appear on your mat?"

Zarad arrived back just in time to hear Angela's comment. "I put it there," he said, laughing.

"If only they could see and hear us," Janel nodded towards the three women. "It would be so much easier for mankind if they stopped looking with their heads and looked through the eyes of faith." She voiced what the other Angels were thinking.

Evelyn stared out at the garden. Somehow her earlier stress felt insignificant. There was something bigger here. Something she couldn't quite touch. It was almost tangible.

Adira put an idea into Christina's head.

Taking a deep breath, Christina reached for the paper again. "Evie, I know you have been really worried about money. I get that. But can't you see, this would solve the problem?"

Evelyn looked at Christina, a big question mark on her face. "What? How?"

Angela took the paper from Christina. "You do realise, Evelyn, that you fit every single criterium here? There is nothing to stop you from changing your life's direction. The only thing stopping you is you. Your mindset. You sit here in what has become too much for you." She held her hand up as Evelyn started to interrupt. "No, let me finish," she said. "Evie, you have to ask yourself. What is keeping you here? What is to stop you from moving on?"

Opening her mouth and then closing it again, Christina hesitated, then taking a deep breath, she said, "Just thinking out loud here. If you take that job, it answers all your needs. You rent the house out, and the money from the rent pays for the taxes and the maintenance. It means you get to keep the house, but more importantly, you won't be alone anymore, and I know you have been lonely."

Buying herself time, Evelyn picked up the coffee pot. "More coffee?" she asked the other women, her voice wobbling a little.

"You can't deflect us that easily. We know you too well," Angela gave Evelyn her stern look. "Evie, Christina has some excellent points. Why don't we pray about it right now?"

"Sure. Yes, of course." Evelyn conceded. The truth was, she was afraid. Afraid of change. Forty years in the same situation had become all she had known.

The four Angels became animated as the women reached out to the Lord with their hearts, lips whispering love praises. One, then the next, and lastly, Evelyn talked to their Father, asking for guidance, asking for Wisdom.

Wisdom smiled as their requests reached her. She despatched a courier angel to activate the first of the gifts she had placed in Evelyn's path.

Unseen, pure light filled the space as the Lord Himself knelt before Evelyn, holding an open vial.

"Oh, can you smell that?" Christina exclaimed, "It's roses, beautiful sweet perfume of roses. I've smelt that before when the Lord was close."

Evelyn started sobbing, her tears falling onto Jesus' hands. He stroked her greying hair, comforting her, and whispering into her heart, until suddenly, she saw the way forward.

Jesus held her as she cried. The scent of the roses all around them both. Pointing at Angela, he said, "Release that word now."

"Evie, I feel I need to say this to you. 'You are my sweet heart. I know your faithfulness even when it has been so very dark. But now I set before you a path. You have asked for Wisdom, and I will give it. Put your hand in mine, and we will walk this together. This path I have created for you'," Angela stopped speaking.

Evelyn's sobs became louder, the years of heartache breaking apart into cries of relief. The darkness of mourning had broken.

The four Angels bowed low in the presence of God the Son. Holiness shimmered around the three women, clothing them in otherworldly radiance.

Gently and quietly, the palpable presence of God and the aroma of roses lessened, lightened, gradually fading away, leaving blessing behind.

The Angels stood, their faces still shining with glory.

Evelyn sighed and took up the newspaper yet again. "I will do it. I'll apply," she said. "I will answer this advertisement." Taking a deep breath, puffing her cheeks out to release the tension, she said, "Now, who is going to help me declutter forty years of memories?"

CHAPTER SIX

Having wrestled through the night with her decision, Evelyn pulled her courage around her and called each of her children. Their responses varied, but all were positive. It was her youngest son, Christopher, who brought it sharply into focus. "Mum, even if it doesn't work out, you still have the house; you are not stuck. If it works out, then you have the start of something fabulous. It's not as though you are old. You have at least another ten years before you want to even think about slowing down." He paused and cleared his throat. "I haven't said this before, Mum, but you are truly inspirational. Even though I do believe in God, I don't have the same faith as you, but it's your faith that helped me get through Dad's death. Because of your faith, I believe."

Thoughtfully, Evelyn hung up. Tears of great joy flowed freely. That her youngest now believed, just because of how she lived her life, was overwhelming in its revelation. *Thank you, Lord,* resonated in her heart all that day.

Janel scooped the joy tears up and handed them into the other realm, where Holy Spirit took them to Father and Son, and they laughed with such joyous abandonment, for another one had found their way home to them.

Evelyn sat in the ensuing silence following the phone call she had just had. The woman on the other end of the phone had seemed very friendly but very professional. Her application for the Grandmother position had been received, and now she had a time and date for an interview. The momentary excitement was quickly doused by anxiety. Her heart rate went up, her throat closing in choking panic. Janel watched, her compassion emanating in waves, but she had to allow Evelyn to make her own choices, to trust the Lord or give in to her fears.

"How many years is it, Lord, since I went for a job interview? I never thought I would be in this position again," Evelyn whispered.

The answering peace assuaged the panic.

She turned her computer on, checking emails and messages on her social media account. Michelle popped up on the chat window. "Just checking in on you. I had this real urge to pray for you. What's happening?" she asked.

If anyone knew the upheaval Evelyn's decision would bring, it would be Michelle. She had not only settled into a new town, made new friends, but she had moved half a world away to Ireland.

"You wouldn't believe what's been happening here," she typed back and then told her the whole story.

"Well, you can only try, Evie," Michelle responded. "It seems quite obvious to me that you have had an angelic visitation, and if that's the case, and it all checks out, could this be Jesus' answer to all your prayers?"

Evelyn sat for a long time that night, considering all the events of the past few days, thoughtfully taking it all apart, seeking for the chinks in the chain of events. There were none. None of it was possible without God.

Since answering the advertisement, new determination gave her purpose, and she started to de-clutter. That seemed to be the new word. De-clutter. *How does one declutter memories, Lord?* she smiled at the thought, *How will I even start?*

"Lord, help! What if I don't get the job, and I'm going through this process! What am I doing?" Momentary panic fluttered through.

Janel drew her sword, and on seeing light, panic fled.

Angela and Christina made the work easier with their laughter. There was so much nostalgia, every little item attaching itself to Evelyn's memories. It was Christina who came up with the solutions. "Every item goes in one of three piles," she said.

"Keep. Maybe, and either give away or throw away."

The women sorted room by room, with the 'keep' accumulation considerably larger than the give-away heap, but the downstairs was finally finished.

❦

Janel rode in the car with Evelyn, Bahadur of the warrior angels flew overhead, his sword ready for combat, but all was quiet.

As she pulled into the driveway, Evelyn took in the beautiful garden surrounding the large house. A mature Jacaranda tree in full bloom stood in the middle of the freshly cut lawn. The gorgeous blue flower canopy stretched towards the sky, mingling the azure colours together. As her car bumped over the cobbled driveway, the jostling gave flight to the already jittery butterflies careening around in the pit of her stomach. Her hands gripped the steering wheel tightly as she anxiously scanned for the front door.

"If my nerves get any worse, I'm going to choke," she muttered to herself. "Girl! Pull yourself together. They won't eat you."

She grabbed her bag and got out of the car, shutting the door and pressing the lock on the key fob. The car obligingly beeped its 'lock' tone.

A man in an old t-shirt and grubby jeans came

around the corner from behind the house, pushing a wheelbarrow full of weeds with a garden fork balanced on top. The man stopped when he saw her and raised a hand in greeting.

"Hi, you must be Evelyn," he called, and setting the wheelbarrow down, strolled over to her, arm extended, ready to shake her hand. A dog hobbled alongside in a strange manner.

Janel raised her arm in silent salute to the angel Asriel, who was following the man. Asriel nodded and smiled. Zarad joined them. He loved it when a plan came together. "We are so excited that this is all coming together, and Keziah sends her greetings."

Evelyn walked towards the man, getting ready to shake his hand, but the dog with the odd gait decided instead to demand her attention. As she bent to pet him, she noticed his strange hobble was caused by his only having three legs. She straightened up in surprise.

The man smiled. "This is Toby. We adopted him as a puppy, as he was going to be put down because he was born with the deformity. Niccola wouldn't hear of it. She was adamant we take him."

The man wiped a hand over the sweat dribbling down his face, leaving a path of dirt from his hand.

Evelyn laughed. "Um, I suggest you go look in a mirror."

"Huh?" The man looked confused.

"You have wiped your muddy hand over your sweaty forehead," she giggled, "You could grow carrots in that amount of dirt."

"Oh! Right. Well, you'd better come around the back with me, and I'll hand you over to Niccola while I get cleaned up."

The butterflies in Evelyn's belly had settled down to a slight flutter, with the man's easy and friendly manner paving an informal path for the interview.

He led her around the back of the house and opened a door that led into a large laundry room. "Nic. Evelyn is here." He called to the house.

Evelyn stood a bit nervously, wondering whether to go into the house or wait in the laundry.

Toby walked between the two of them, ambling jerkily on his three legs, and disappeared through the doorway. Evelyn waited, unsure as to what she should do. Stand and watch the man wash, or follow Toby? She decided to at least step into the doorway. It felt awkward watching a complete stranger wash, even if it was only his head, arms, and hands.

The laundry room led directly into the kitchen. Large and wonderfully fitted out, Evelyn felt a bit intimidated. Would she be expected to cook for the family? How would she even begin to master the bewildering array of electronics that stared at her with their bright lights?

"OH!" A voice startled Evelyn. A petite dark-haired woman with olive skin stopped abruptly on seeing a stranger in the kitchen.

Evelyn flushed in embarrassment.

"You must be Evelyn," the woman said smiling. "Josh, where are you?"

"Ah, he's in the laundry washing up. I encountered him when I arrived, and he brought me around the back." Evelyn looked around the kitchen appreciatively. "Nice kitchen. It must be wonderful to have all this counter space."

The woman's answering smile lit her face up. "It's such an awesome kitchen. I'm a messy cook, so this allows me to spread out everywhere. It's the cleaning up that's the problem," she laughed. "Anyway, I am Niccola. I'm so glad you are here. Would you prefer tea or coffee?"

Instantly Evelyn's nerves melted away, put at ease by the love behind the friendliness.

Abaigael nodded to the other angels from her place by Niccola. "There is a battalion led by Bahadur stationed around the perimeter," Zarad told them. "Our Lord deems this assignment to be very important."

With coffee made, Niccola led Evelyn into a beautiful lounge room. Evelyn chose a seat where she could see the room and look out into the garden, with the Jacaranda tree standing proudly. A familiar sound of praise music was playing, embracing them both with its quiet beauty.

Suddenly, Janel and Abaigael reached for their swords. Zarad flew out. The disturbance in the atmosphere was potent. Janel went immediately to Evelyn, with the other two angels guarding Niccola and Joshua. Another attending angel immediately disappeared to help Eliora protect Arabella.

An aberration rippled through the atmosphere, and Evelyn and Niccola both tensed, their spirits picking up on the anomaly.

Janel stood guard over Evelyn.

The women mentally shook themselves.

Abaigael and Janel both sighed with relief and sheathed their swords.

"I will never understand how people just cannot see and hear what we do." Zarad walked through the wall and re-joined the group. "It's true, isn't it? Every time the enemy tries to strike, if the people of God will only praise Him, it gives us the strength to put the enemy to flight." There were nods of agreement. The music wove its praise through the atmosphere, leaving notes of refreshing and droplets of glory wherever it was heard.

"What incredible power the Lord has imbued mankind with, that their very words and acts of praise and worship cause such a shift in the spiritual realms."

Asriel followed Joshua as he strolled into the room.

"Hey! Where's my coffee?" Josh stared at the tray in mock accusation. "That's ok; I know my place. I'll go get my own."

Niccola called after him, "Honey, I know you don't like cold coffee, so I didn't pour it for you. Besides, you know where the coffee is kept." She giggled and rolled her eyes. "Men!"

Evelyn laughed. It had been so long since she had seen this sort of loving interaction between a couple. It was a delicious and refreshing reminder that married love and laughter were still around.

Toby settled with a contented grunt at Niccola's feet and groaned in doggy appreciation as she scratched his belly with her foot. "Josh is a veterinarian. I couldn't let him put the puppy down," she said. "Too many animals are destroyed because they aren't perfect. And yes, Toby's breeders may not have been able to sell him, but that doesn't mean someone wouldn't love him. He's a Labradoodle, a cross between a poodle and a Labrador." She looked at the little dog who was slowly closing his eyes, three legs in the air, little snuffling snorts as he eased into sleep.

"I wonder what animals dream of," Evelyn mused. "We had a cat when the children were young, but since David died, it has felt too hard to invest emotion into anything except getting through." Her eyes grew large as she digested what she had suddenly just understood.

Josh came back with his coffee and settled into what was obviously his favourite chair; long legs stretched out in front of him.

"So," Evelyn said.

"So," Niccola echoed. "Yes, I suppose we

should talk, shouldn't we, although Evie, you don't mind if I call you Evie, do you?" she looked at Evelyn questioningly. "You seem like an Evie to me."

"Evie is my preferred choice, actually. David always called me Evie, and all my friends do. So yes, please. Evie is very nice."

Niccola beamed a brilliant smile at her. "Well, as you realise from the advert, we need someone to help us to look after our daughter. Both Josh and I work long hours, and it's becoming more difficult to juggle our schedules to accommodate Bella's needs. With Josh being a vet, sometimes his shifts are erratic, and I own a food manufacturing business that necessitates some international travel, especially for trade fairs."

Evelyn shifted uneasily. "Er, would I be expected to cook for you? I'm not a chef; I've only cooked for my family and friends."

Niccola blinked at Evelyn's obvious anxiety, and in sudden understanding, said, "Oh! Oh no, Evie. I'm not a chef. My company does condiments. Um, chutneys, sauces, that sort of thing. No, you don't need to worry about cooking gourmet meals! But yes, let's talk about that right now. Most nights, we are both home by around 6:30 pm, and it would be so very lovely to have a home-cooked meal waiting. You know the sort of thing, maybe a roast one night, BBQ in summer, just family meals."

Evelyn nodded. "Yes, I can do that easily, I think."

Joshua leaned forward in his chair, his face animated, and asked, "Will you make us puddings and desserts?"

"Oh, Josh!" Niccola laughed at him, "You will turn into a pudding if you eat like that all the time."

"Mmmm, pudding," Josh rubbed his stomach and pretended to drool.

They all laughed.

"Well, I guess that's settled then. Josh wants puddings, occasionally." Niccola smiled as she picked up a file. "Right, I've got a list of things here that we need to discuss. Evie, tell me about you. Tell me who Jesus is to you."

As the three people talked and got to know each other, Janel, Abaigael, and Asriel listened. Zarad flitted in and out, checking on the perimeter patrols, and vanishing into the Heavenly realm, only to reappear again. "Arabella has asked the Lord for a special request. I have to ensure it happens," he said and disappeared again.

"You mentioned in the advert that the successful applicant would have a separate cottage?" Evelyn thought she'd better clarify. After being on her own for so long, the thought of living in a house, no matter how large, with three comparative strangers was daunting.

A cell phone disturbed the conversation. Niccola glanced at the phone as it flashed its blue light.

"It's my sister," Niccola said. "Excuse me a minute.

"Hi, Bronnie. May I call you back? Yes, yes, we are in the middle of it now. Yes, ok. I'll call you later." Niccola ended the call. "Bronnie is eager to know if you are 'the one'," she gave a small laugh. "Now, where were we? Oh yes, your cottage. We can go and have a look at it soon." Niccola was very much in charge here, very much the company CEO running an interview.

'Moww.' Evelyn was startled by the demanding tones of a Siamese cat. "*Meayowl, maoww.*"

Josh clicked his fingers to the cat that had just stalked into the room. "Come here, girl."

The cat ignored Josh and minced her way very delicately and deliberately towards Evelyn. Her tail waved sinuously, counterbalancing each serpentine step.

Zarad guided the cat, talking to her, giving her instructions. The cat continued its mincing, meticulous walk and jumped straight up onto Evelyn's knee. Woman and cat eyed each other. Zarad nudged the cat, and very pointedly, the cat put her front paws on Evelyn's shoulders, and there, cat and human sat, eyeballing each other.

"Well, hello, puss," Evelyn said, stroking the silken chocolate coloured fur. "Aren't you beautiful?"

"Mummy, Daddy. This is the right grandmother!" A young voice came from somewhere behind the cat, for Evelyn could see nothing beyond the feline face.

"I asked Jesus for a sign, so we would know which grandmother to choose."

A young girl plonked herself on the arm of Evelyn's chair.

"Hello. I'm Arabella. You must be my new grandmother. Thank you, Jesus, for telling Saffie to do that." Arabella looked at her parents. "I asked Jesus to show me which grandma to choose by getting him to tell Saffron to jump up onto the right grandmother, and look her straight in the face because animals know, don't they, Dad?"

"Yes, honey. Animals do know," her vet father answered his daughter.

Picking Saffron up and putting her on the floor, much to the cat's disgust, Arabella then slid off the arm of the chair so that she was wedged in tight with Evelyn. "I'm going to call you Grandma," she announced. She then got up and pulled Evelyn out of the chair. "Let's go and look at your house. I love your cottage."

The Angels started yelling and dancing. "Mission accomplished!" shouted Zarad.

CHAPTER SEVEN

The steam from the tea curled up aimlessly.

Six weeks of unrelenting pressure; packing the house up, deciding which furniture to keep, what to redistribute, and what to store. Evelyn had chosen to take only a few pieces. Much of what she and David had collected over the years was very worn. This was a new season, and she knew she couldn't drag the old around with her. Many of the knick-knacks the children had given her when they were young had been boxed up and given back to them for their own memories.

Niccola and Evelyn had worked together to empty the cottage of the furniture Evelyn would replace with her own, and the new tenants would be moving into Evelyn and David's house next week.

It was the closure of an era, and now she sat in her chair, in her new home, the last of the unpacked boxes staring at her, demanding her attention.

Tears trickled slowly down her face; her mind yearning to be back in her familiar place, the comfortable place. Panic filled her, and her heart started racing, a cold sweat covered her body, and she gasped for air. "Jesus," she cried, "Jesus, help me. Lord, I just want to go home!" Choking sobs and gulping agitation.

Janel was moved with compassion, but knew she had to stand by and let Evelyn push through the panicked anxiety and find her own peace in the Lord.

"Take a deep breath, girl," Evelyn instructed herself. "Slowly, breathe slowly. Have a drink. Trust in the Lord and lean not on your own understanding." she quoted the well-known scripture. The panic eased back, sweat drying, as her heart rate lowered to normal. She reached out a shaking hand for her tea and sipped it; little sips, deep breaths.

"Lord, I'm sorry. Look at me. The minute you put me into different circumstances, I revert to wanting my old place. Just like the children of Israel in the desert." She was disgusted with herself. "Wow, Lord. Where did that come from? I think you are exposing what's in my heart. I don't like that!"

Taking her empty cup and saucer to the kitchen, she stopped and looked out onto her private courtyard. *What a beautiful space,* she thought, *I have been so very blessed.* Evelyn opened the sliding door and stepped outside. She had been too busy to really explore the area and now spent a few minutes in delight, looking at the flowers and shrubs and then exclaiming out loud when she found an empty garden bed.

"It's new. We built it for you because we know you like gardening." Niccola had walked quietly up to the courtyard. "I brought you some dinner, as I didn't think you would be up to eating with us tonight. Besides," she laughed, tossing her dark hair out of her face, "It's all I can do to stop Bella from running straight over here and setting up house with you."

"That's thoughtful of you. Thank you," Evelyn gave Niccola a quick hug. "What if I have the next two hours to myself, time to eat, and then perhaps Arabella might like to come over, and we'll start to get to know each other?"

Niccola nodded. "She would like that. I bet she suggests she stays the night in the guest room. But shall we have some coffee now? It would be nice for just the two of us to sit quietly."

"Oh, I absolutely agree. Come on, then. I'll put the coffee on, and you get the cups and tray ready. We'll sit out here."

༶༶༶

Keziah, Habib, and Zarad had arrived in the War Room earlier than the appointed time. There was a sense of expectancy among them. Other Angels came in, their joy contagious at this new assignment of the Lord's. The buzz of melodic voices spilled over into the ante-room, where the guards kept vigil.

BANG, BANG, BANG.

Three times the guard's halberd thudded on the ground. Immediately, there was silence. The King was coming in. All Angels bowed low.

The King of all Kings walked into the War Room. A roar of praise exploded from the Angels, joy dancing across their faces, rippling into the outer fringes of heaven where others caught the beauty of the notes and joined in.

Habib hurried to catch the spontaneously uttered praise, his quill scratching speedily across his scroll.

> We give praise to the King
> In the council of the upright
> and in the assembly
> The deeds of the King are great
> Greatly desired by all who enjoy them
> His work is full of majesty and splendour
> and his righteousness continues forever

In A Capella style, their voices harmonised, weaving in and out of each other, growing louder into an upwardly spiralling crescendo, abruptly stopping in a glorious finale.

Jesus, the King, took His seat at the head of the table. The meeting was convened.

"You have followed Arabella since her sending forth from my Father's heart," He said. "Eliora has watched over her faithfully, with Abaigael and Asriel guarding her parents. Janel has been with Evelyn, and Evelyn's husband, my friend David, has sometimes watched with me. When my precious ones graduate from earth to our home here, it is very difficult for those whose walk is not yet finished. I couldn't take Evelyn yet. Her life's scroll is still being read; all the prophesies my Father spoke over her are yet to be fulfilled." He paused to give Habib time to write all that was said. "Now is the appointed time. All the training and discipling Evelyn has undergone, is now about to be birthed into this marvellous plan for mankind."

A murmur rippled across the assembly. None but the Three-in-One knew what the assignment was.

Jesus smiled at them. His eyes sparkled mischievously. He knew they were all eager to know what would happen next and how it would impact and surge, swelling across and out through all eternity.

"We; my Father, the Holy One, the Spirit of God and I, being in one accord, and as one, have decreed that this child whom we named Arabella, would carry a sword in one hand and my word in the other. She has been anointed since before her conception for this work." He parted the curtain between the realms and talked directly to Eliora, Janel, Abaigael, and Asriel. "You have been faithful. Well done. Now your work is about to be increased. I will send help when you need it, and your people will be guarded. Warrior Angels who have been instructed to do perimeter watches are being despatched, and also to increase the personal watch over each of the Beloved."

The Son looked around all the assembled Angels. "This is the time of the great awakening. You have all been working for a long time getting prepared. I have seen your deeds. I have seen the Hosts getting ready for the in-sweeping. You have been getting into your formations, ranks, and positions. We are on the cusp. The stage is set. I have many Arabellas and Evelyns in strategic places. You are to protect them. They are to remain hidden. Their work in destroying enemy lines is too important for them to be exposed until the appointed time. I will personally meet with them, and they will be given their mandates that will bring principalities crashing down and usher in my Kingdom on earth, as it is here in Heaven. Do you have any questions? Anything we need to further clarify?" The Lord looked around and gave the Angels time to formulate their thoughts.

Habib was still busy taking notes of the meeting. They were important documents that would be filed in the annals of Heaven's library. If ever the Accuser called one of the Lord's people to court, the documents would be brought forth before the Righteous Judge. A true and holy record, crimson with the blood of the Lamb, which would then refute the accusations.

Yairel bowed to the Lord. "My Lord. I have wondered about the woman Evelyn. She is just and righteous. She is made holy by your blood. But I cannot see the anointing on her that you have placed in Arabella?"

The King smiled at Yairel. "I named you well, Yairel, for as your name means 'enlightened one,' so you like to be. Eve you all know. For from Eve came all life, so the second part of my daughters' name Evelyn, tells the rest. Lyn being a cascade or a pool beneath the life-giver. Thus, we have Evelyn. The source of life with the refreshing of the pool. For every Arabella, there is an Evelyn. They were made to work together. The mother who gives nourishment to the sword-bearer."

There was an astounded murmuring followed by praise for the wisdom of God.

The Son left the room, and the meeting adjourned.

CHAPTER EIGHT

"Grandma, I'm home," Arabella announced loudly as she dashed upstairs.

"Hello, lovely girl," Evelyn called back. This was their daily ritual; Evelyn's signal to boil the kettle for her cup of tea and get milk and snacks ready for Arabella.

The weeks had flowed into each other with late Spring unfurling her greenery towards summer. Evelyn became more comfortable in her new life. The kitchen in the big house was a constant source of delight, from the gorgeous granite work tops to the abundance she discovered in the gardens, and the large, well-stocked butler's pantry gave her such joy. Providing delicious meals for her new family without worrying about the rest of the week was a relief and contrast to all the years struggling with financial constraints.

"Grandma, guess what?" Arabella dashed into the kitchen, a junior tornado whirling and twirling her way to the kitchen counter, pulling out a bar stool and plonking herself onto it.

Evelyn smiled at her young charge. "What,

honey?" she answered, patiently waiting as Arabella appeared to inhale her glass of milk rather than drink it, and shoved a whole cookie into her mouth.

Arabella wiped her mouth with the back of her hand and burped. "Oops, sorry," she giggled, then added seriously, "But do you know what I found out today? My friend Becky wants to come and live with us."

Evelyn put her teacup down carefully. "Excuse me? What do you mean Becky wants to come and live with us?"

"Her parents are getting a divorce, and Becky has to choose whether to live with her mother or father. She doesn't want to choose. She wants them to be a family. So, she said she will come and live with us because we are a family." Arabella grabbed another cookie and thoughtfully nibbled around the edge of it. "You don't mind, do you, Grandma? We have a big house, and Becky's parents go to our church, so we know them."

There was a sudden heaviness in the room as Evelyn grappled with understanding what Arabella had said. They went to their church but wanted to divorce? What? *Lord, how can they bring such dishonour on you? How can they tear themselves apart like that!* Evie silently prayed, and clearing her throat, said, "Err, I think that's a question you need to discuss with your parents. It's a big decision to make. But why don't we pray for Becky and her family?"

Arabella jumped off her barstool, rushing to

hug Evelyn. "I knew you would understand, Grandma. I told Becky you would, and I told her we would pray.

Eliora and Janel became animated with joy as they prepared to catch the petitions and decrees and take them before the King.

Xenus stepped through the wall, his usually serious face even more determined. He held a scroll in his right hand and unrolled it. "The child, known as Arabella," he said, reading the words on the scroll, their life dancing with light. "Is now ready to begin the next stage of her training. She holds the sword of the Lord in one hand, and the decrees of life in the other. This is her first assignment." He touched the scroll to Arabella's head, and then placed it into her heart. Bowing to the other Angels, Xenus left again.

"Grandma, I know what I have to pray for Becky and her parents." Arabella was suddenly very serious. "It's strange because I was going to just ask God to make the family happy again, but it's as though I've suddenly been able to see what is happening." she appeared to grow, her Spirit gaining maturity that had not been there before.

Nodding, Evelyn silently stood up. She closed her eyes and quietly began to give glory to the King of Kings.

Janel lifted her face to the realm of the Creator. There was no house anymore, no earth; they were in the time between time, the place of the Spiritual reckonings.

Arabella stood quietly for a moment, her child-like face suffused in joy as the Holy Spirit of God Himself wove a vivid rainbow of effervescence around her. She raised her right hand and, tilting her head back as though to be able to see into Heaven, started praying, "Lord God, Becky's parents have sinned. They have torn their hearts apart and believed a lie. For your purpose in marriage on this earth is to reflect your love for us. Forgive us all, Lord God, for we have believed in the things of man rather than your truth."

The sword of the word of God arced a lightning rod into the spirit dimension, with an answering firebolt reverberating through the heavenly realms. Eliora and Janel fell to their knees in awe of the power of God. Hordes of demons shrieked as Michael and his troops launched into attack mode.

Gabriel stood and, in a thunderous voice, declared, "You intended to harm the people of God, but God intended it for good to accomplish what is now being done, the saving of many lives."

The clashing of swords and the howls of demons being put to the sword, roared, reverberating through eternity.

In earth's territory, Arabella lowered her arm. "In Jesus' name, I declare restoration of that which has been stolen. I ask for you to put Becky's family back together again." The intensity showing in her eyes faded, and the warrior again became a child.

"Amen," Evelyn agreed with her. "I am sure that we are going to hear good things now, Bella. I know that God heard us. Now, give me a hug. I haven't had a hug today, and then I have to start dinner, and you have to do your homework." She smiled at the girl she had come to love. "And then you need to walk Toby."

Arabella nodded. She felt quiet, as though she was on the verge of discovering a great cosmic secret, something very holy, something out of her grasp that if she spoke would dissipate.

Eliora and Janel were just as quiet. They had known their assignments were sacred, but they had not fully realised who Arabella was in the Lord until now.

"We must double our vigilance," Janel said. "If the nameless one finds a foothold, he will use it. We knew this child was destined; we just didn't know what for." Eliora nodded.

"I am in awe that the Lord God would give me this assignment. Almighty God, I praise you. You are wise and beyond my understanding," Eliora raised her voice blending in with untold others, all glorifying the God who was, even before they were created. She saw the great crowd of witnesses dancing before His throne. The Angels prostrated themselves on the Crystal Sea, as the Son, He who is in the form of mankind, but also God, walked among them.

Great holiness pervaded the kitchen in the earth realm. Evelyn hummed a favourite chorus of praise while Arabella did her best to understand her maths homework.

Life sped by, and it seemed it was only days, not weeks later, as Evelyn watched Becky's parents in church sitting close to each other, smiling, touching hands. The epitome of fresh love. There was no more talk of Becky coming to live with the family. Evelyn smiled to herself. "Lord, you are so good," she whispered.

CHAPTER NINE

Toby sleepily opened one eye, his nose sniffing out the gathering in the lounge room. The darkened room grew in intense brilliance, and Saffie blinked in the light as she minced down the stairs to investigate what it was that had woken her.

The mingling of delicious aromas swam through the house. In other rooms, the sleeping occupants dreamed of flowers in meadows and exotic spices, sweet orange and myrrh.

Arabella stirred in her sleep, her mouth moving in soundless words.

High overhead, the gathering was noted and reported back to headquarters. The Prince of the Power of the second heaven was not pleased.

Those who had come to the meeting ceased their excited chatter as Gabriel arrived. They bowed to him in respect, and he bowed back, for to honour others is the highest mark of esteem.

Eliora, Janel, Abaigael and Asriel were at the front of the gathering. Their robes glistened, shimmering with the colours of Heaven.

Saffie stalked into the middle of the assembled Angels and sat there, calm and self-assured that she, as the cat, would be welcome. She also had been given her assignment for this family.

Gabriel smiled. "Cats. How many have sat on the Lord God's knee? They show yet another side of His love. I'm sure if a cat could, they would push the Almighty off His throne." The Angels laughed. They knew the assured nature of a cat was just a reflection of the Creator. Saffie yawned as though already bored with this conversation.

The scroll in Gabriel's hand became illuminated, and he unrolled it. "As one who beholds the face of Almighty God, I am privileged to bring this message to you all. Many of you were present at the time Arabella was called forth to come to this world. You heard the prophesies spoken over her, and you," he said, nodding towards Eliora, "have been faithful. Arabella is now poised to leave her childhood behind and enter the arena of confusion; that time where she is no longer a child, but not yet thinking with an adult's mind. This is a critical time. As you know, the Lord has given each of mankind the ability to make their own choices. Either to choose to follow the Lord God or to slide into the ways of the evil one.

"Arabella is being trained by the Spirit of Almighty God, the blessed one of the throne of the Lord. We know from our information gathering that the evil ones are seeking her destruction. But," and Gabriel looked very serious as this revelation hit those in the meeting, "The Almighty has decreed that no matter what decision Arabella makes, not one hair on her head will be harmed. You can expect distractions, temptations, the spirit of rebellion, the lusts of the flesh, to all come and try to pull her from her original assignment. If she chooses to stay true to the Lord God, her name will resound through eternity, and she will pave the way for others to follow. If she doesn't so choose..." Gabriel shrugged, indicating too many others who had been down that path before. "The nameless one has demanded to have Arabella that he may, by inward agitation, try her faith to the verge of overthrowing it."

There were gasps of dismay at this statement.

Gabriel held his hand up for silence. "But, our Lord Himself has prayed that her faith will not fail, and when the sifting is over, that she will stand."

Grunts of acknowledgement that the Lord's words held more sway over the Angels than the words of dismay. They thought back to another one whom the nameless one had tried to subvert. It hadn't been successful.

"Gabriel, what are the limits of our jurisdiction when it comes to Arabella dealing with these temptations?" Eliora asked. "How far are we allowed to intervene?"

Janel put a hand up. "Gabriel, Evelyn has had much experience with young people, having brought up her own three children, but none of them held the anointing this child has. Will you be sending us reinforcements?"

A low murmuring from among the Angels rippled around the room.

"Evelyn will be given Wisdom when she asks for Her help," Gabriel answered Janel. "But we are not allowed to intervene in mankind's free will. Your authority will be limited to keep her from physical harm should she choose to follow the enemy's path. However," he paused and grinned at them. "However, we have a secret agent. Saffie is imbued with a particularly stubborn streak, and the Lord can and does use animals to influence humans."

Saffron stretched and yawned, and then walking over to Gabriel, she slowly blinked her blue cat-eyes at him. Her answer was obvious. '*I understand.*'

"Thank you, Saffron. We are glad to have you on our team." The Angels laughed. It wasn't the first time the Lord had used animals to prompt humans to take a different path.

Gabriel flew back to the Throne Room, and the Angels dispersed. The aromas wafting through the house gradually diffused, leaving but a hint of what had taken place. Toby snorted and settled back to sleep. Saffie walked up the stairs together with Eliora, who took her place by the bed; Saffie jumped on the bed, and both guarded Arabella.

Janel stood by Evelyn's bed and silently asked that Wisdom be given to this beautiful Grandmother.

Abaigael and Asriel stood in the lounge room for a while, the silence broken only by Josh's light snoring. They smiled at each other and together went back to watch over their sleeping humans.

※

"Knock knock," Niccola called as she came across the lawn to Evelyn's cottage. "I come bearing gifts." She came through the courtyard and into the kitchen. "I bring an offering of carrot cake."

Niccola's cheeky grin made Evelyn laugh. "You have won my heart forever, and I will willingly do your bidding. I love carrot cake," she said, dramatically licking her lips. "I'll make the coffee, and you take the cake outside. I think it's warm enough," she said, peering out the window at the sky.

Late spring was warm but often raining. Today, however, they were lucky. The sun shone brilliantly, and the courtyard was alive with the spring growth, bulbs flowering, the roses just at bud burst, all creating a glorious shout of colour and perfume.

Niccola sat back in the outdoor chair, her face tilting to the sun's warmth. She kicked her shoes off and wriggled her toes. "Josh has taken Bella to Becky's place, so I'm using this time for some subterfuge. Do you know that my little girl is going to be a teenager soon? And she's going to go to high school? It scares me, Evie."

Reaching over and taking the younger woman's hand, Evelyn just nodded. She had gone through it three times, and it would appear she was about to embrace the teenage years again with Arabella. "Oh, I understand, alright!" she exclaimed. "What were you thinking of doing for her birthday?"

Niccola yawned and stretched. "I thought about a pool party. We can put the BBQ on at about 2 pm, the girls can swim, eat, and then their parents can come and get them at around 6 pm. I don't think I could handle a gaggle of girls for much longer than about four hours."

Evelyn chuckled. "You don't think you are going to get away without a sleep-over, do you? My advice? Start the pool party later in the day. Limit Bella to no more than six friends and then say because it's a sleep-over, the girls must be collected by 10 am. Oh, and ensure that Josh isn't on call that weekend!"

"Oh, wise one. Yes, you are right," Niccola leaned over and kissed Evelyn on the cheek. "I'd better get back before the whirlwind arrives home. Thank you, my new mother, for your love and wisdom. Oh, and before I forget," she stopped, "I have a trade fair in February, just before Bella's birthday, so I will need you to help me out with this. Please! Can you imagine if I left Josh to handle it?"

Laughing, Evelyn waved her away, "Of course. As if I wouldn't help! You'd better go and have some alone time while you can."

Doing a quick twirl, Niccola chuckled. "I hear and obey, oh great one."

"Nicely done, Janel," Abaigael called back as she hurried after her diminutive charge.

CHAPTER TEN

"Byee, Byee, Bye," Arabella yelled, excitedly hopping from foot to foot as the last of her birthday guests left. Slamming the front door shut, she scooped the cat into her arms, thumping up the wooden stairs, her hand trailing on the bannister.

"Bella, don't slam the door," her mother called.

"Sooorrrry," she called back.

"I'm a teenager now," she sang. "Teen neen neen een. Do you know what, Saffie? I'm a teenager now. You aren't a teenager, Saffie. You are a cat. Cats don't get to be teenagers." But the cat was not interested in whether Arabella was a teenager; all she wanted was to be free. She did not want to be constricted by an overexcited girl.

"Ow, Saffie, that hurt! Get down," she said as the cat struggled for freedom, clawing Arabella's arm as she tried to jump free. "I don't need you, Saffron. I'm a grown-up now," the girl called as the cat ran out of her bedroom.

She flounced onto her bed. "Teen, neen, neen, een" she said again, listening to the rhythm of the sound. "I don't feel different. Am I supposed to feel different? Yesterday, I was twelve, and now I'm thirteen. That makes me a teenager. I'm grown up now. Teen, teen, teen." she tried the sounds again, rolling onto her side and yawning widely. It had been such a fun night, but there hadn't been a lot of sleep with her friends there for the sleepover.

Arabella yawned again. Teenager or not, the child Arabella was tired from her sleepless night. Her eyelids fluttered, and soon her breathing slowed into a gentle, rhythmic pattern as she drifted into sleep.

Eliora smiled in amusement at Arabella's mouth working in her sleep, her mind processing her day.

Downstairs, Niccola sat thoughtfully, holding her coffee in both hands. How could her baby have now entered into the teen years? Where did that time go? "Lord," she prayed. "Protect Bella through these choppy years. Father, cover her, protect her, bring her safely through." Quietly she made her way up the stairs, stopping at her daughter's bedroom door. She leaned against the door frame, taking in the innocent beauty of her sleeping child. *Teenager, you are still a child.* Niccola's thoughts meandered through 13 years of joy.

Upstairs in his office, Josh stared out the window, seeing nothing at all, looking far into the future. How would Arabella handle the storms of the next few years? He had done all he could to equip his precious daughter for this turbulent time. "Jesus, look after my daughter. I entrust her to you, for there is nothing more I can do now except pray. Give us wisdom, Lord."

Evelyn wandered around her courtyard garden, her ever-present cup of tea in hand. Her thoughts flitted around her three children's teen years, some easy, some really hard, and she prayed that God would guide them all.

In a meeting room in another realm, Angels gathered together. Keziah called the meeting to attention. "This meeting is now in session. We are here to talk about the child named Arabella. She has reached an important milestone in her life, and while she is yet a child, we are aware of plots from the evil one. Plots that, should they succeed, will destroy the child. The Lord God, blessed is His holy name, has decreed that the enemy can influence her, but he cannot touch her physical body. We know of plans to destroy her child-like faith before it reaches maturity and to pull her into great sin."

Dismayed murmuring spread among the Angels. Much discussion was had until finally the course of action was set, and Keziah dismissed the Angels back to their duties, Eliora, Janel, Abaigael and Asriel back to their people.

CHAPTER ELEVEN

The time of birthdays and that early first teen year merged seamlessly, with a smile remaining perpetually on Arabella's face; the time of childhood fading slowly into that of the time in which to grow up. Gradually, she seemed to shed the skin of the tender years of childlike innocence through the year, with the young adolescent taking shape instead.

Niccola and Joshua had braced themselves for the often-tumultuous years of the early teens. Still, if anything, Arabella seemed to be maturing right in front of them without any real problems.

Saturday morning in early summer, the family sat having a leisurely brunch. Those times were rare. Joshua was not on call, and Niccola didn't have to be at any market or trade fair. It was family only.

"I want to be baptised," Arabella suddenly announced with her fork halfway to her mouth, the scrambled egg falling off it.

Like an exaggerated pantomime scene, everyone stopped and looked at her.

"I mean, I've been thinking about it a lot. We've been going to church forever; I know Jesus, and I know this is what He tells us to do, so I want to be baptised," she reiterated.

Eliora looked at the other three angels. Her face broke into the biggest smile, delight manifesting just as dust motes do when the sun's rays fall on them. The kitchen suddenly seemed a lot brighter.

Josh folded his newspaper and carefully laid it on the table. Absently he placed his left hand on the paper while his right hand stroked his chin—an act showing the depth of his emotions.

"Kiddo, that's wonderful. Isn't it, Love?" he glanced at Nic.

Niccola jumped up from her seat and embraced her daughter. "I'm so proud of you, Honey. To follow Jesus is the only way through this life. Yes, we absolutely support your decision. And like Paul said to Timothy, don't let anyone despise your youth. You talk to Pastor Bernie tomorrow."

"When I get baptised, I'd like Aunt Bronnie to come as well."

"Sure, I'll call her," Niccola nodded her agreement.

Shovelling the rest of her egg into her mouth, Arabella jumped up from the table. "I'm going to tell Grandma," she called back over her shoulder as she ran to Evelyn's cottage.

Her parents sat in silence. Joshua had his head

down, and when he looked up, Niccola noticed the glint of tears in his eyes. She put her hand over his—unspoken communication, affirming what was in their hearts.

Eliora danced around the kitchen, giving great leaps of joy, and much to the amusement of Abaigael and Asriel swooped up through the ceiling and flew at speed back through the house wall. "YES!" she shouted. "Yes, she is taking that crucial step."

The following day at church, Arabella opted to sit with her parents instead of with the other young teens. She was very quiet, seeming to look inwards, as though absorbing through every pore in her skin the words Pastor Bernie was saying. As he closed the morning service, blessing everyone and dismissing them to enjoy the rest of the day, she stood along with the congregation, with an almost fierce quietness in her spirit.

Arabella stood off to one side, waiting until Pastor Bernie had finished with all the others who wanted to talk to him. Lauren saw her, and with her usual big beautiful smile, came over.

"Hey, Bella - how ya going?"

Lauren was one of Arabella's favourite church people. She walked with a crutch, and sometimes her speech was difficult to understand. But oh, her heart was magnificent, and Arabella always felt so loved by her.

"Look!" Lauren handed her crutch to her and proceeded to walk six steps unaided. "I've been practising, and Jesus is walking with me. I can feel him right by me." Her excitement was palpable.

Arabella watched in awe. Grandma had explained why Lauren walked strangely and why her speech was a bit strange. Grandma said Lauren had had a stroke. *Whatever that is,* Arabella had thought.

"I want to be baptised, Lauren, so I'm waiting for Pastor Bernie."

Lauren did a little jerky half hop and reached for her crutch. "I'm so excited! Bella, that is awesome." If there was one thing that Arabella absolutely loved about Lauren, it was the way in which she never treated her as a child but always as an equal.

Arabella took a step closer to Lauren. Lauren immediately reached out to her, enveloping her in a one-armed hug, her other hand holding onto her crutch.

Extricating herself, Lauren smiled delightedly. "I have to go now, Bell. But I'm going to phone you later, ok?"

Niccola stood a distance away, watching her daughter's interactions, a queer mixture of sadness at the child rapidly disappearing, and joy at the young adult emerging.

Finally, as the last of the people trickled out the door, Arabella walked over to her Pastor.

"Pastor Bernie, may I talk to you?"

He smiled at her. "Of course, Bella."

"I want to be baptised."

The true heart of the man showed on his face, delight followed by joy. "Bella, that brings me great happiness. Let's go and find Mrs Walker, shall we?"

They walked into the church kitchen, where Diane Walker was chatting with some women as they cleaned up after the service.

"Diane," Bernie got her attention. "Excuse me, ladies," he said to the others. Drawing his wife aside to a more private space, he put his left hand on Arabella's shoulder. "Bella has told me she wants to be baptised. Would you please arrange to take her through what baptism means? Then we will schedule it for next month."

The diminutive Diane Walker appeared to a casual observer as being quiet and unobtrusive. But to those who knew her, she was a warrior, enormous in the sight of God. "Bella, it would be my great pleasure to talk about what Baptism means." She drew the young girl away to a quiet space, making plans to meet weekly after Sunday services.

∽⟐∾

"Grandma, I've been looking up the verses Mrs Walker gave me about baptism." Arabella sat in her usual place at the kitchen counter. Evelyn had her back to her, peeling the vegetables for dinner.

"Mmm-hmm," was Evelyn's response. She

knew to give Arabella time to process her thoughts.

"Well, it's like there are so many different things about being baptised. Mrs Walker told me to look through the four gospels and read how John baptised people. It all seems to show that you have stopped sinning. Look, see," she said, jumping off the bar-stool and taking her Bible over to Evelyn. "Look, Mark 1 verse 4 says, 'And so John came, baptising in the desert region and preaching a baptism of repentance for the forgiveness of sins.' But look at this, Grandma," She flipped through the pages of the Bible. "Here, look at this."

Evelyn put the vegetable peeler down, washed and dried her hands, and took the book. She read where Arabella was pointing. *'We were therefore buried with him through baptism into death in order that, just as Christ was raised from the dead through the glory of the Father, we too may live a new life.'* (Romans 4 verse 6). Evelyn raised an eyebrow in query to the girl.

"Don't you see, Grandma! It's more than just to say to everyone, 'I am following Jesus now.' Every verse that Mrs Walker told me to look up is just..." she trailed off, unable to express with words what her heart was seeing. "Just so ... alive... it touches me... and oh, how I wish I could explain, but I don't have the words. I just know that something happened when I read it."

The many Angels in the kitchen bowed low, for they knew very well what Arabella was struggling to say. They had watched, all those years ago, as the Son of Man, himself, went through the waters of baptism and then the baptism of extreme suffering.

Holiness rested in the kitchen. Thoughtfully, Evelyn turned back to her dinner preparation. Arabella stared out the window, looking at nothing, but seeing everything inwardly, as revelation unfurled in her heart.

Each week, Mrs Walker took Arabella step by step through the scriptures on baptism, confident in her pupil understanding the giant leap she was about to take. At their last session, the Sunday before the date set for her baptism, Mrs Walker had her Bible opened at an Old Testament book.

"Today, we are going to look at the ancient roots of modern-day baptism. By modern, I mean from John the Baptist onwards." She looked down at her Bible. "Have a look at Joshua 4 verse 9: '*set up twelve stones in the midst of Jordan, in the place where the feet of the priests which bear the ark of the covenant stood…*'," she read.

Arabella looked confused.

Mrs Walker continued, "You see, when the children of Israel left Egypt with Moses, they had to undergo a type of baptism when God held the waters of the Red Sea back. But later on, when they had to cross the Jordan River, the Lord held those waters back again. In Joshua 3:15, we read that the Jordan was in flood. The Lord had told Joshua what to do and how to do it. If you read through the entire chapter, it sets out the baptism of the entire nation of Israel through the Jordan river, which, it would appear, is the exact place where many years later, John baptised Jesus. Joshua told the priests to *'Take up the ark of the covenant and pass on ahead of the people.'* When the priests got to the edge of the Jordan River, as soon as their feet got wet, the Lord stopped the river from flowing, and the water piled up high. Joshua then chose twelve men representing the twelve tribes to follow the priests carrying the Ark.

"When the priests got to the middle of the river, they stopped. All the people of Israel passed by them and made it safely to the other side of the river. Joshua told the twelve men to each take up a large stone from the middle of the river, right where the priests were standing, stones big enough so that they had to carry them on their shoulders. The men had to take the stones to where they were all going to camp that night. He said, *'These stones are to be a memorial to the people of Israel forever.'*

"There is so much symbolism here: the priests carrying the Ark of the Covenant, which of course, symbolises Jesus; the twelve representatives being the sign of God's government; the stones from the middle of the river, where they had been sitting waiting to come out of the waters that had flowed over them for who knows how many centuries. And then finally, as the stones came out of the water, they were to be a memorial for all of Israel, that

God had brought them from death to life."

It took Arabella a while to process what Mrs Walker had just told her. "So, what you are saying, is that Israel was symbolically baptised at both the crossings, the first time with Moses and the second time with Joshua. And then the stones were to mark the place where they all crossed over into their new land?"

"Yes, Bella, that's exactly what I'm saying. But there is even more in this chapter of Joshua. If you read the second part of verse 16, '*It piled up in a heap a great distance away, at a town called A'dam in the vicinity of Zarethan.*' It could be argued that Adam founded this town after he and Eve were told to leave Eden. So, therefore, we see the baptism of Israel going all the way back to Adam. Nothing in the Bible is a coincidence, Arabella."

Bella's face screwed up as she tried to understand what Mrs Walker was saying.

"If we will only think with an enquiring mind, Arabella, we will find so much more that the Bible infers, but because of our lack of understanding of the Hebraic ways, we completely miss it. Adam is represented as a type of remorseful sinner. He is described by Rabbi Avot de-Rabbi Nathan, who lived around the 8th century, as fasting, praying, and bathing in the river for 47 days as a sign of repentance for his sin." Mrs Walker smiled, "I know it's a lot to take in, but I will write it all out for you so you can read it again. Okay, we'll leave it here. I so appreciate your desire to truly know Jesus." She hugged Arabella, kissing her forehead; their last meeting before her baptism.

A few days later, Aunt Bronnie arrived.

"Hello, Sweetie," She called, spying Arabella looking out her bedroom window. The girl waved excitedly, and Bronnie could hear her thumping down the stairs before the front door was yanked open, and a mini-tornado sped out to grab her aunt in a hug. Bronnie bounced her way through life, and to Arabella, that seemed very exotic and intriguing, full of life.

"Next to Mum and Dad, and Grandma, you are my most favourite person in the world." She grabbed Bronnie's hand, half leading, half dragging her into the house.

"Oh! Well, I'm honoured," Bronnie laughingly said.

On Sunday night, more than ever before, Arabella felt the presence of Jesus. She raised her head, eyes closed and drinking it in. Bronnie sat quietly during the service, observing those around her.

"And now, what we have all been waiting for," Pastor Bernie smiled at the congregation. "We have four people wanting to be baptised."

Arabella, along with the other three, walked to the front where the tank of water stood waiting.

"In Acts 2:38, Peter was speaking, saying, '*Repent and be baptised, every one of you, in the name of Jesus Christ for the forgiveness of your sins.*'" Pastor Bernie got into the tank, and his wife Diane helped

Arabella get in.

"1 Peter 3:21 says, *'And this water symbolises baptism that now saves you also—not the removal of dirt from the body but the pledge of a clear conscience toward God. It saves you by the resurrection of Jesus Christ.'* Arabella, do you believe that Jesus Christ is the Son of God, that he died and was resurrected on the third day?"

She nodded her head; the moment seemed so solemn, so sacred that there were no words to express her thoughts.

"Then, I baptise you in the name of Jesus."

As Arabella slid under the waters of death, the Angels were waiting to receive her, stripping off her old garments. Jesus, Himself, gently laid her body aside, for she was now dead to her old life. He saw his own image in her and dressed her in a new garment, shining, woven in the very reflection of Himself. Kissing her forehead, he breathed His new life into her. She stepped inside Jesus, to abide in Him forever.

Arabella rose again out of the water, a new creation, her old self lying dead in the water.

The Angels looked on as the dead Arabella lay in the waters of baptism, the new life now clothed in Jesus Himself.

"'*I am confident of this, that he who began a good work in you will carry it on to completion until the day of Christ Jesus,*'" Pastor Bernie spoke truth over her, "Arabella, may your heart and your spirit hear this word and respond."

As the word of God was spoken as a decree, the other realms shook. Truth shot out as a flaming arrow, straight through the demons who had gathered to destroy Arabella, scattering them and sending them reeling apart. Screams were heard as Truth shattered lies. Truth continued her journey, straight to the Son of God, landing gently in His hand, melding to become one with Him, He who is truth.

CHAPTER TWELVE

Discordia faced the grotesque creatures in front of her. "How could you allow this to happen," she screamed at them.

"Discordia," ventured a tiny demon, "You know that as soon as they speak Truth, we are undone."

"Stop it, STOP IT. I don't want to hear that name." Discordia slammed her hands over her ears. The other demons did likewise, shutting their eyes, all babbling furiously to drown out the sound of Truth, the sound of The Word. The sound of the name of He who had paraded them as a defeated army before all of Heaven. "You, Wee-Evil," she said, pointing at the tiny demon. "Get Trivia. Tell her to do what she is best at. Get that child to do ANYTHING that will give us legal access to her life. Anything, do you hear me?"

The tiny demon bobbed up, shuffling out as fast as he could, trying to get back into Discordia's inner circle with this errand. He fluttered, his wings not strong enough for him to soar, stumbling and wobbling midstream as he plummeted through territories, eventually coming to Trivia's domain. Full of his mission, he strutted into her court, darting between the feet of those in her court seeking to kick him. The atmosphere reeked of spells and curses, an acid green hue colouring the air. Trivia's book of shadows hovered near her chair, the pages turning freely by themselves. Her concentration was fierce as she peered between dominions and empires.

"Trivia," the runty demon called out to her, what brains he had, submerged under his own self-importance as he dodged those feet, pushing his way towards the witch.

Behind him, Trivia's sycophants gasped at his affrontery. Trivia stopped mid-spell, the slime green atmosphere crashed to the floor.

"Who are you?!" she lashed out, pointing her finger at him until he levitated and hovered, squirming, off the ground. "How dare you interrupt me. Who let you into my kingdom?" Trivia hissed, globules of spit spraying out of her mouth. She lowered her hand abruptly, causing the demon to crash to the ground.

Undaunted, he got up and strutted over to her, his cognisance of the situation minimal. "Discordia wants you. You are to go and see her immediately."

"Oh, she does, does she. Why didn't she come and see me herself?" The witch turned away and suddenly swung back. "Just who do you think you are, coming and demanding from me? ME! Who is she to demand I go and see her! Get out of my way, you little turd," Trivia kicked the demon to one side, causing him to roll off into a dark corner. Swirling in a chaos of darkness, Trivia disappeared, reappearing in front of Discordia.

"Well, well. The little globule of snot actually got you to come." The two once beautiful angels circled, each assessing the other to see who was the stronger. "Let us put aside our differences," purred Discordia. "I have need of you, an assignment you will no doubt enjoy immensely."

"Oh, you have *need* of me, do you? Enough to give me some of your dominion?" Trivia asked. "Two can play this game. What is it you want of me? It had better be very very g-g-g. ARRRRGH! I can't say that word." She held her head, her eyes bulging. "It had better be extremely vicious and nasty," she hastily changed her wording.

Discordia purred back at her, "VERY vicious and nasty. Oh, very. For this is such a plan as to upset Heaven. Even HE will be forced to take notice of our power."

The witch stood a little taller, her interest piqued. "Upset HIM? Why, Discordia, why didn't you tell me?" Trivia hissed while shape-shifting rapidly from witch to demon, from demon to an innocent-looking human, innocence giving way to a kaleidoscope of distorted shapes and colours, and back to witch. "Show me my assignment then. I can't wait to get started."

CHAPTER THIRTEEN

Jesus swung the gate open to His own private garden. No one was allowed in there unless He invited them. He wandered around the paths, touching this leaf, kissing that flower, talking with the birds and small animals who fluttered and skittered around, adoring him. Butterflies landed on the end of his nose, making Him laugh. He made for His customary place by the pool, the small lake—His own still waters. The reflection of the glory emanating from the City in the North, danced on the water, sparkling its praise and love.

"Father," He said. "Father, I endured all the torture and shame of the cross for the joy set before me, and now, Abba, I reap my reward. My beautiful ones, redeemed and brought back to you." He smiled. "Did you see Arabella, Abba?" He listened to the answer, unheard by any other. "Yes, I agree. Just as you prophesied over her before her conception. So shall it be."

"My feathered friends, my little creatures. Thank you for your love and care of my garden. Now, I must meet with some other friends." He smiled at the creatures and walked through the garden, back through the gate, instantly reappearing in His council room, where the Angels were waiting.

The meeting was now in session.

"This is where the child enters her training," He said. "Where those things, that my Father prophesied over her, are firmly embedded into her very being. Honed, cut from living stone, steel, and sharpened." He turned to where a chart was hovering, with glowing living letters. On the chart, the aspects of Arabella's life, the prophesies, her faith, hummed with a frequency that was tuned to that of Heaven, while her human flaws hung covered in blood. Precious blood. Tapping the chart, Jesus said, "We are here to talk about Arabella becoming a son." He chuckled at the use of the word 'son' in connection with a female. "Yes, this is something we have covered many times, and we will cover again and again, for mankind is still earth-bound, and many remain embedded in the things that are only of the physical realm. Son always means a child who has attained maturity. There is no longer male and female. For they are all one in me."

The angels laughed, for it was indeed true. They were bewildered about mankind's seeming obduracy over the spirit realm that was so very real, and yet many of mankind just could not, or perhaps would not see it.

Habib was writing furiously, capturing every word that issued from the mouth of God.

"Since the time of the Judges in Israel," Jesus said, "men have sought to subjugate women. I put a woman, Deborah, as Leader and Judge over the people. And by referring to my daughters as 'sons', I deliberately challenged the traditional mindset and raised the status of women to their true design."

Jesus smiled at them all, fully understanding their perplexity, before turning his attention back to the chart on which Arabella's life was glowing. "Since time began, the nameless one has done everything he can to subjugate women, for my Father put enmity between the nameless one and the woman. As a baby, I was born of woman, and from and through me comes salvation to all creation."

This great mystery led to an endless discussion amongst the Angels, as they sought to know the mysteries of God, which were given only to man.

As the discussion about Arabella took place, the angels discussed Arabella's baptism, how her old self had been left dead in the water, and she had risen again, just as Jesus had.

He looked intently at the Angels. "The witch Trivia, is going to try to take Arabella off course. Trivia, a perfect name for her, mimicking the demon goddess Diana, the spawn of Nephilim.

"She will try any witchcraft she can, oh, very subtly. But I am in Arabella, and she is in me; therefore, my Spirit will warn her. Be aware at all times. Protect her from physical harm, but in the end, she must make her decision herself. Eliora," Jesus turned to Arabella's Angel, "You know what to do."

"Yes, Lord." Eliora bowed before the King.

"Now, let us talk about the path she is to take. As she is still young, we have a lot of work to do. Her training will be intensive. Time is short." He turned to Janel. "Janel, you have been faithful in your service to me by guarding Evelyn for so many years, but her assignment is not yet finished. She is integral to our purposes. Ensure she is encouraged. Adira and Duriel, your mandates remain the same; that Angela and Christina remain close to Evelyn."

The angels nodded. Droplets of fire rapidly spread from head to head, until the room was ablaze with the manifested spirit of praise; the glorification of the Lord who was so passionately involved with each of His beloved, so much so, that he even knew when a tiny bird died. The room lit up with a flash as their praise opened thresholds. The frequency quickly spread until all Heaven's realms rang with His praise.

Eliora took a deep breath of the atmosphere, the gilded presence of God, so tangible in Heaven. As she translated from Heaven to Earth, she released the breath of presence over Arabella. Dancing, swirling, glistening rainbows glimmered around her, settling as burnished golden light in her hair, falling onto her shoulders and landing on the floor as precious gems, unseen in the physical realm.

If Arabella had been able to see it, no words in earth's dictionaries would be able to express what it looked like.

And all Hell shook.

CHAPTER FOURTEEN

Bella was conscious of a difference in her life, a freshness as though she had woken from winter into the glory of late spring. Her Bible readings came alive, almost like the characters danced off the pages. She carried a small Bible in her school bag and read it whenever she could. An insatiable hunger grew in her to know and understand more; the more she learned, the more she shared with her friends, whether they wanted to hear or not.

As Arabella drank in the written word of God, so Eliora also learned, for angels do not know everything. With Holy Spirit revealing more to Arabella, the angels looking on longed to know more, and as they did so, Eliora and those around Arabella also grew.

༺༻

Rage was not a strong enough description when Discordia's spies informed her that Arabella had died and was reborn through the Blood. Her stinging and cruel hatred created barbs, which pierced any demon and evil spirit who was unfortunate enough to stand too close to her.

She spun anti-clockwise and, much to the relief of her minions, disappeared.

Trivia was in the middle of spell casting with an open portal between realms. A coven of witches could be seen through the vortex. As the witches uttered their evil, the spirits under Trivia's domain flew through the open portal and straight into the humans, inhabiting their bodies and minds.

Discordia ignored Hell's protocol. She strode straight up to Trivia, taking hold of her spell-casting book and dropped it to the floor. "You told me you had this Arabella mission under control!" she screamed. "You have completely failed!"

At the interruption of the spirit flow, the open portal collapsed. The human witches' powers dissipated, leaving them confused, the stench of evil, all that remained.

At Discordia's fury, Trivia's demons cringed, pushing and shoving to be out of the way of what they were sure would be a violent scene.

In the earth realm, humans became anxious without understanding why; their ability to read the spirit realm almost zero. Arguments broke out between lovers. Dis-ease infiltrated normally calm people. Those who could, read the portents and completely failed to understand. Only a few who were Kingdom walkers sensed the battle going on between two principalities.

Discordia and Trivia stood motionless, each

eyeing the other for the first move, weighing their options to overpower the other.

Trivia saw her opportunity to knock Discordia off balance. "Now Discordia," she purred, "the plan is working beautifully. You have not understood. Perhaps your powers of observation are failing you? Mmm?" she taunted.

"Just how is letting Heaven increase their Kingdom on OUR earth falling in with your plans? Or maybe, you are seeking to atone for your fallacious deception all that time ago in Heaven? Traitor!" Discordia screamed.

Trivia smirked at Discordia, "Oh, you really don't understand, do you? Poor Discordia." Trivia's disparaging comments bit into Discordia, appearing as barbs in her back. "Maybe, I will ask his majesty, the great Lucifer, if I should take over your portfolio?" Heaving a dramatic sigh, Trivia put her arm around Discordia's shoulder. "Listen to me. Let me explain, as you so obviously do not comprehend all that is at play. My assignment, the one *you* gave me, remember? The child, Arabella, is completely unschooled in the matter of us!" The 'us' coming out as a hiss. "We who hold all the power and dominion. I have it all planned out, Discordia. When she is sufficiently lulled into her childish security, believing that 'He' will save her, then my plan will be activated."

Looking sceptical, Discordia pulled away from Trivia's claws, which were digging into her shoulder, her grasp getting stronger, seeking to subjugate her opponent. "And just what IS your plan? I am unconvinced and fully prepared to go before the council and report your ineptitude. You have one earth month, Trivia." She spun around, seeming to evaporate in tendrils of black vapour.

CHAPTER FIFTEEN

"Hi," Arabella dumped her bag on the ground by her friends. "I don't like maths. Why do we have to know why $A - B = Y$?" Arabella pulled her lunch out of the bag. The morning maths and science classes had addled her brain, and she just wanted to chill for a bit. As she sat down, the conversation stopped abruptly. Puzzled, she looked at the faces in front of her. Sophia looked away, clearly uncomfortable. Jerrah whispered something to Lexie.

"What?"

Jerrah sniffed. "Nothing. We're not talking to you."

A spiteful demon slapped Jerrah across the head.

"Jerrah is having a party, Bella," Sophia blurted out and then immediately looked at Jerrah guiltily. "Sorry, Jerrah. It just slipped out."

"A party? When? What's it for?" Bella asked, looking to Jerrah and back at Sophia.

Jerrah looked annoyed. "It's just a party. You're not invited. We don't want to be around you with all your churchy stuff." She stood up. "We're sick of you ramming God stuff down our throats," she yelled as she haughtily walked away, her entourage following.

Sophia followed, looking back remorsefully at Arabella, who was watching them leave, completely bewildered by what had happened.

Two demons danced around chortling in vicious glee. "We did that well. Trivia won't kick us now," one of them whined.

It was a very different Arabella who got off the school bus that afternoon. She had tried to talk to Jerrah but was ignored; her efforts at finding out why Jerrah was being so mean completely failed.

Miserably, she dropped her school bag in the hallway and went into the kitchen to find Evelyn.

"Hi Grandma," was all she could manage before the tears started and her throat closed, with just the sounds of rejection choking out.

"Sweetheart, whatever is the matter? What's wrong?" she put her arms around the girl, slowly rocking her from side to side, patting her back.

Arabella desperately tried to regain control. Never in her young life had she been so rejected. As the story sobbed out, Evelyn could feel anger surging inside, like that of a bear's need to protect her cubs. Grappling to control herself, she silently prayed, "Lord, help!"

Jesus stood in the kitchen. Eliora and Janel knelt before Him.

"And so, the training of the young lioness begins." He placed a hand on each of the Angels' heads. "Here, give this to her." Jesus handed Eliora a leaf from the Tree of Life, which grows by the river flowing from under the throne. "As she sleeps, I will visit her in her dreams."

The leaf from the Tree of Life was placed into Arabella's heart that night, its healing reaching into her mind as she slept.

She kept to herself at school, finding a quiet place at lunchtime to sit alone and read her Bible, gaining comfort from its beauty. She would sometimes see Sophia looking at her pleadingly, but Bella ignored her.

Arabella spoke up in the Saturday night youth group, speaking of her school friends with whom she'd openly shared about Jesus; her expectation being that those who went to church youth group with her would understand and be excited in her passion for Jesus.

Keagen Brown looked at her. At 18, he was one of the older ones. His mother was involved in any group she could get into. "Not everyone shares your enthusiasm, Arabella," he drawled her name out. "Most of us have more adult things to talk about." He yawned and stretched. "Anyway, I have to leave you now; I am going out later."

Keagen's pride and arrogance left the room with him.

Arabella felt as though she had been slapped in the face. A child who didn't understand what had just happened.

The youth group leader was left stunned, completely unprepared for these dynamics. "I think we'll leave it there for tonight. See you all tomorrow at church." Jan quickly prayed, closing the evening meeting. "Bella, oh, I don't know what has got into him. Are you ok?"

The young girl just nodded, and gathering her stuff, hurried out of the church after Becky to catch a ride home.

Letting herself into the house, instead of bouncing into the lounge room as she would normally do, she just called from the hallway, "I'm tired, I'm going to bed. Night."

The shower poured its comforting streams over her. She whispered, "Lord, I don't understand. Why did Keagan say that? I thought he loved you too."

Watching from the other realms, Trivia hissed in demonic pleasure. "I told you I had a very good plan, Discordia," she sent the telepathic message. "We will take as many down with us as we can, and she is a prime target."

In spite of the wounds inflicted the night before, Arabella woke in the morning, eager to go to

Church. Her young life was centred around her church family, and her happy place was in the time of worship. She never hesitated to speak of her passion for Jesus, willingly praying openly and sharing her joy, unafraid to talk about what the Lord was showing her at that time.

On the way into the building, she saw Lauren, and skipped up to her, giving her a fierce hug, which almost unbalanced the older girl. Lauren playfully swatted Arabella with her walking stick, and they both laughed. "You are so awesome, Bells. I love it when you do stuff like that. Everyone else thinks they have to be so careful around me, in case I break!"

She didn't notice Keagan's mother, Mrs Brown, looking at her in a disapproving way.

While Arabella loved all there was about her church, she loved Sunday evenings the most, when the services were centred around worshipping the Lord. The angels in the church joined in with the congregation as they sang to the Lord, with Arabella lost in the ecstatic presence of the Lord, her arms raised in adoration.

Eliora and Janel dove in and out of the streams created by praise and worship to Almighty God. The music Angel looked at them and smiled, while the Angel of the Fellowship glowed, as the soaring notes and humble hearts glorified the Lord. Angel after angel rode the flow.

Janel nudged Eliora. Something was jarring; something seemed to feel wrong. They both looked around uneasily. Something had entered the building, something that didn't glorify God. Both angels slowly scanned the people, looking for infiltration.

Eliora motioned to the Angel of the Fellowship. He looked to where she was pointing. Over by Mrs Brown sat a Gossip Demon, poking his fingers into her eyes, forcing her head to glance, and look again at Arabella. He whispered into her ear and darted around the other side of her head to whisper into her other ear. Another spiteful spirit was gleefully banging on Keagan's head.

As though the people could see what was happening in the spirit realm, the praise and worship suddenly fell flat. The musicians floundered to the end of the song. It all felt confusing.

Mrs Walker sensed the shaky atmosphere and bowed her head, praying. Pastor Bernie walked to the lectern and indicated to the musicians to stay where they were. "Let's just sing in our prayer language, shall we?" He nodded to the lead singer to start.

As the sacred prayer languages rose together with the notes filtering through the air, the Angel of the Church was given the authority he needed and confronted the gossip and spiteful spirits. "You have no right to be here. You must leave."

Gossip sniggered. "Oh no, we don't have to leave. She," it said, pointing at the woman, "She has invited us. We will stay."

Pastor Bernie tried his best to labour his way through his sermon, but the atmosphere the demons had brought hung heavily, banishing freedom. Finally, giving the benediction and blessing all who came, he sighed with relief. The service was over.

Arabella started making her way to the rear doors of the church building. Mrs Brown caught up with her. "Just a little bit of advice, Arabella, dear," she said, her condescending tone giving lie to the use of the word 'dear,' "If you were a truly Godly girl, which I have no doubt you think you are, dear, I would dress somewhat differently." She indicated Arabella's jeans and sneakers. "Godly girls wear dresses; they dress modestly. Oh, and another thing. I know you really like my Keagan, but you aren't his type, dear." She turned away. "God bless you, dear," she threw over her shoulder as she walked over to her friends.

"That's good, oh that's good!" Gossip congratulated himself.

Spitefulness nodded his agreement. "Oh yes, Trivia will be very pleased with us. Very pleased."

Eliora held her sword up, protecting Arabella as she hustled her out of the rancid atmosphere.

CHAPTER SIXTEEN

Michael strode into Trivia's domain, his sword ready and the presence of God shining all around him. "He knows about your plans, Trivia. You will not succeed."

All her treachery in Heaven rushed back, reminding her that God would never forget. She cowered away from that presence, every droplet of it burning her.

"Go away," she shrieked. "Get out of my dominion. You have no right here."

Michael smiled knowingly. "Oh, but you know that the Lord God has every right to be everywhere and anywhere He chooses. And right now, He chooses me to warn you. He knows your plans." Michael hovered between the second and third heavens, pausing long enough to warn her again. "That which you have meant for evil, the Lord God is turning to His glory and Arabella's good, to bring to pass, to save many people."

The sudden brilliance as he ascended into the true Heaven momentarily blinded Trivia. She shuddered, slumping to the floor.

The days seemed interminable as Arabella dragged herself unwillingly to school each day, not wanting to face those whom she had thought of as friends. She felt alone, shut off and shut out. Home was her safe place. On Thursday morning, she ignored her alarm when it rang. Bed was safe. There were no mean girls here. If only she could stay in this cocoon forever.

Downstairs, Niccola and Josh spoke quietly, perturbed at the sudden change in their daughter. "Let's leave her for today. We'll tell the school she's not well and then talk to her tonight," Josh made the decision. "I'll call Evelyn and let her know."

Arabella stayed in her room where she felt secure, only leaving when her parents insisted that she go to school on Friday. A young, frightened girl sitting alone at school that day. Ostracised.

The demons threw themselves on the ground, laughing at her distress.

"Mission accomplished," they hissed gleefully.

When Sunday came around again, a day that Arabella had previously been overjoyed to celebrate, she was very hesitant to go to church.

"Don't take any notice of that woman," Niccola said about Keagan's mother. "She's a gossip and a busybody. She needs to mind her own business.

Dad and I are with you, okay? Now we need to leave, or we will be late."

Arabella had just nodded. Her mother hadn't heard what Mrs Brown had said; and more than what she said, it was how she had said it, as though she were some sort of slut. Her mother didn't know what it felt like. If only she had told her mother straight away. Surely her parents would call Mrs Brown and tell her to mind her business? But what if Mrs Brown was right? She was, after all, an adult and a Christian.

As she walked into church, she felt as though she were in a strange building. It didn't feel right.

Standing alongside her, Eliora was on high alert. She could sense the atmosphere; the stifling demons of gossip had multiplied.

"Bella," Lauren called. "Come and sit with me today." Somehow the older girl sensed her need. "Let me lean on you; I need a human walking stick today." Lauren pushed her hand through Bella's, the touch of love soothing. Eliora followed silently, walking in unison with Courage and Joy. "Bells, look at me," Lauren made Arabella look at her. "Bella, people who gossip are just silly, and they obviously do not know their Bible. Just don't take any notice of them."

A single tear escaped Arabella's rigid control. She stuck her tongue out to lick it off the side of her mouth. "But why, Lauren? I haven't done anything to them. Why are they doing this?"

"They are jealous, okay? Small-minded people who don't know you. But I do. You are one amazing chicky babe, Bells. Don't ever forget that I think you are fantabulous," Lauren said.

Arabella could not lose herself in worship. The evilness of the gossip, the injustice of it stung. And even though, in her mind, she knew it was just people being horrible, she couldn't shake it.

As she sat through the service, an evil spirit, with self-righteousness flying as a banner off its head, looked at her through the eyes of Mrs Brown. A friend of Mrs Brown's kept glancing at Arabella and whispering to her husband. Gleefully, Scandal dug its talons into the woman's head, oozing poisonous thoughts, which she accepted and whispered again to her husband. He looked uncomfortable but did nothing to stop his gossiping wife.

When Pastor Bernie got up to preach that morning, he looked grim. "I want everyone here to turn to 1 Corinthians 6 verse 9, and we will read it together, out loud. 'Do you not know that the wicked will not inherit the kingdom of God? Do not be deceived: Neither the sexually immoral nor idolaters.'" He continued to read, but when he read verse 10, he seemed to put particular emphasis on some words. "...nor slanderers, nor swindlers will inherit the kingdom of God."

The droning from the pulpit just sounded like so much buzzing in Arabella's ears. She tuned it out and did not hear the rest of the sermon. She didn't hear the rest of the verse, that slanderers, which includes gossipers, would also not inherit the Kingdom unless they changed their ways. Arabella couldn't enter into worship or hear the sermon for the intensity of the demonic spirits saying nasty things in both her ears, drowning out the sound of love.

"Turn now to Romans 1:29." The Pastor watched as the people found it in their Bibles. "This is a hard word, but it's in the Bible, so we need to take notice of it." He read through the verse, and when it came to the last part, 'They are gossips and slanderers,' there was a shrieking coming from those demons. They put their hands over their ears, babbled furiously to drown out Truth. And their babbling drowned out Truth over Mrs Brown and her friends with their self-righteousness. But the word of God had been spoken; the demons Gossip and Spitefulness looked scared, ready to flee. Eliora glared at them. The people they were attached to, though, refused to listen, and they grew stronger, even more bold and dug themselves into their human hosts.

"Did you know," one woman said to another later, "that that lovely young man Keagan, had to nearly forcibly push Arabella away from him? She was that besotted with him. His mother told me."

Slander jumped up and down on the woman's head in delight. The spoken Word had fallen onto rocky ground.

The other woman raised her eyebrows in delight, making a mental note to tell her friend that Arabella was turning into a tramp. *Only to pray for her, of course,* she thought, even while knowing it was a lie.

Eliora could do nothing. Her assignment was to physically protect and, when the time came, to guide her charge in the right direction. For now, though, she could only pray.

What used to be a place of great joy, a sanctuary, had within a few weeks become a place to be endured. Arabella didn't stay for the usual chatter at the end of the meeting. She avoided Pastor Bernie and bolted out of the door, waiting by the car for her parents.

Lauren watched the devastating scene with great sadness, but inside her was rising a wave of righteous anger.

And Hell laughed.

But that night, the Lord did as He said He would, and He stepped into Arabella's deep sleep. Arabella became aware of a large dog. The dog came up to her and licked her all over, ensuring she was thoroughly clean. She was completely relaxed, and love was pouring through her. Satisfied with his work, the dog lay down, and Arabella lay next to him, with the dog's right front leg protectively over her. "I love you, my Arabella. You will never be the same again," the dog said. She slept securely, enfolded by the dog.

The alarm drew Arabella out of her sleep, a deep, warm and refreshing sleep. She sat up in bed, stretching, forcing her eyelids open, and blinking at the new day peeking through her curtains.

Filtering back through her sleepy mind came thoughts of how she had felt so safe, so secure. "Toby?" she said. Toby, did you come and sleep with me last night? The little dog came bounding up the stairs at the sound of her voice. Arabella stared at him. "No," she whispered. "No, it can't have been you. The leg that was over me is the one you are missing."

Eliora smiled. Her Lord was at work, and the leaf from the Tree of Life had responded to the frequency He carried.

CHAPTER SEVENTEEN

"Bella, you have to come to church with us. You know the rules. I don't understand what's got into you. Why are you avoiding youth group and church?" Niccola was exasperated.

"I just don't want to go anymore, okay. Just leave me alone. Church is boring."

In the privacy of her room, Arabella curled into a ball on her bed, holding her Bible tightly against her chest, seeking the comfort it used to bring. Her parents didn't understand; no-one understood. It was better not to go, then she wouldn't be hurt, and those horrible women wouldn't say such awful things.

Over the creeping weeks after Trivia's seemingly successful coup, Arabella became restless, easily annoyed. Church and youth group were denounced as boring, her parents as being controlling. Evelyn was increasingly dismissed as irrelevant.

Her restlessness became sporadic anger.

"It's just hormonal, Josh," Niccola tried to reassure her husband. "I've spoken to my friends, and their kids are the same. It seems this is the age and stage." She sighed, running her hand through her hair. "It will pass, Honey," Niccola tried to reassure Josh.

But it didn't just pass.

Eliora continued to do all that she had been commissioned to, but it was no longer enough. The demons taunted Arabella incessantly, mocking her, speaking their foulness into her mind. *'Tramp, useless, unworthy, no one wants you.'* Whatever lies they could whisper over Arabella, they did.

Her dreams were filled with horror. The whispering in her ear made her feel that she was going mad.

Her passion for Jesus became something of the past, and even though in the privacy of her room, she occasionally talked to Him, it wasn't the same as her first love, that time when her heart sought Jesus, revelled in Him. Arabella continued her slide away from her church family but never quite disowned Jesus. On her nightstand, her Bible was opened less and less, and at school, she started gathering a new group of friends.

The new friends she had made at school were not the type of friends Arabella's parents would have chosen for her. Their morals and language didn't line up with the code at home, and it wasn't long before she started to slide into their lifestyle.

As she chose to walk towards darkness, her behaviour grew correspondingly dark. The light that had filled her being was taken over and crushed, subdued by dirty grey.

It was the creeping darkness that eventually pushed Arabella directly into the hands of the enemy. All that Trivia had planned finally reached its conclusion, giving her authority to invade Arabella. She knew the protocol of the spirit realms. She was unable to do anything except upload a barrage of lies over the intended victim until they finally opened a chink in their armour.

Joshua sat in the garage with his head in his hands, unable to comprehend the change in his beautiful, gifted Bella. For eighteen months, Arabella had been hell to live with. *Hell-bound,* he thought. Hell-bound indeed.

Surely, she was still there, somewhere within his angry daughter? All the promise she had shown lay buried in the lifestyle she had embraced. It seemed the more they tried to draw her close again, the worse she got.

With her values and morals being eroded, as she chose friends whom Joshua and Niccola would never have chosen for their daughter, her swift ride down into the shadow world had torn at the seams of their lives.

Arabella was rude and becoming completely uncontrollable. Rude to both him and Niccola. Rude to Evie. They were anxious for Evelyn. She had not signed on to deal with this. What if she decided she'd had enough? What if she left? He groaned. "GOD!" he cried to the empty garage. "Lord, where are you? We desperately need you." He felt that his cries seemed to echo through the rafters, hit his car, and bounce off the garden equipment, but unseen, they were gathered into the Lord God's heart. Joshua's heart and mind roiled in anguish, words spinning through his inner turmoil. Words he was unable to voice.

Saffron stalked into the garage and wound herself around Josh's legs, purring loudly, then suddenly jumped onto Joshua's knee, bunting his chin, and forcing his head up. She eyeballed him. "Saffie, how is it you know what we humans need?" He stroked the cat's silken coat. Saffron's blue eyes stared intently at the distraught man; then, she seemed to turn her head and wink.

Asriel laughed. "Good work Saffron," he told her. The cat gave her big contented cat smile, then curled up and promptly went to sleep. Asriel continued his watch over Joshua. There was nothing he could do until the man lifted his mouth in praise to God.

It was Kilynn's birthday that changed everything. All Arabella had been taught was still held in the sacred secret place inside. But the need to belong and be accepted was now greater than her early upbringing. Reluctantly, Niccola and Josh had agreed to let their 15-year-old daughter stay over at Kilynn's place for her birthday.

Full of birthday food, the girls went upstairs to

Kilynn's room.

Deception sniggered and whispered into Kilynn's ear.

"It's too early to sleep!" Kilynn jumped up. It's only 10 o'clock. Let's play some spooky games.

Eliora stood right in front of Arabella and pleaded with her to run, get up and run. Go home. Get out of here. The back of Arabella's neck prickled, her almost-submerged, Holy Spirit conscience sounding alarms, but she pushed it down, ignoring the warning. Her loneliness pushed aside caution.

"Let's do Red door, Yellow door," Mia said, "Let's do that first."

"What's that?" Arabella asked.

Mia looked surprised. "Haven't you played it before?" She asked. "You lie down on someone's lap, close your eyes, and we all say 'Red door, yellow door or any other colour door'. You will see things. It's really spooky. You go first then, Bella."

Eliora ascended quickly, looking for help. Jesus met her, sorrow marking his face. "I know. She has to make her own choices," He said.

"OK," Arabella said, "but you will have to tell me what to do." She lay on the floor, one of the girls moving to cradle her head on her lap. The five remaining girls started the chant: "Red door, Yellow door or any other colour door."

Again and again, they spoke the evil incantation.

"I choose the yellow door," she said.

Arabella felt as though she was being transported, floating through a door of emptiness, an absence of breath and hope. She was powerless to stop, powerless to voice the silent scream as faces of wickedness rushed her, running right through her as though she wasn't there.

Trivia manifested her human form, beckoning Arabella closer and closer and closer, stroking the girl's hair, pulling her into her trap. The yellow door of fear.

A blinding flashing light broke the trance. Arabella screamed, gasping for air. The other five girls all stared at her. "Bella, Bella. Are you ok? What happened?"

Shrieking, Trivia withdrew. The violence of Michael's sword caught her off guard. "Remember, Trivia. The Lord knows your plans. This is His child."

"I don't want to play that anymore. No, no." Arabella was panicked. Her hands compulsively pulled at her hair, face white and tense.

Suddenly, Kilynn jumped up. "I know. I'll get my mother's Ouija board, and we'll play with that. I'll get candles as well, so it'll be really creepy."

Eliora rang every alarm bell she could, but Arabella closed them down, her need for acceptance greater than the fright from which she had just escaped.

The girls sat on the floor with the Ouija board in front of them, the glass in the middle. They lit two candles, so the room was in near darkness, with just enough light to see the board.

Six girls each put a finger on the glass. Arabella's heart was hammering. She knew this was wrong. Eliora was desperate and called on the Lord. "She has to make the choice, Eliora," He told her.

Kilynn talked to the glass, asking the spirits to talk to them. The glass moved violently as a demon pushed it from letter to letter, spelling out its message.

ARABELLAISMINE

Arabella stared at the message that had been spelled out. "This is freaky. I don't want to play this. Actually, I want to go home."

There was a lot of gloating in the second heaven that night. Trivia's witchcraft had won.

Or so she thought...

CHAPTER EIGHTEEN

At Arabella's screaming, Niccola ran up the stairs faster than she had thought possible.

Her daughter was standing in the middle of her room, pointing at the window. "I saw it. I saw it," was all she could get out.

"Saw what, Honey? What are you saying?" Niccola looked to where Arabella was pointing. "Oh, dear God. Lord God, what is that!?" she stared at the three slashes on the outside of the window.

"Mum, I saw it. I saw it doing that."

"Come downstairs with me, Honey. I'll get Dad, and I want you to tell us what you saw." She hurried her daughter out of the room and downstairs. "Josh," she yelled. "Josh, come here now!"

"What's wrong?" he asked as he came into the kitchen. Niccola pushed him to the whimpering Arabella.

Joshua cradled his daughter, holding her tight. "Ssh, Baby, ssh, tell us what happened." He led her over to the table, gently pushing her into a chair.

"Daddy, I saw it. Please don't make me go back in that room. I don't want to go back into my room." Her fear made Josh's arm hairs stand straight up. It was his job as her father to protect her. But protect her against what? He glanced at Niccola as she put a hot chocolate in front of Arabella.

"Ok, Bella. Have some of your drink. Now, tell us what happened."

She took a sip of her drink, gaining some control over her emotions. "I was doing my homework when I thought I heard something, so I looked out the window, and there was a horrible thing outside. It dragged its claws down the glass. You have to believe me. Go and look. The claw marks are still there."

Josh was worried. Had whatever scared his daughter excavated her mind of sanity? "I'll go and look, Bella, okay? We're here now. You're safe."

Taking the stairs two at a time and hurrying into Arabella's room, he was struck by the cold atmosphere in the room, and then he saw the window. Yes, Bella was right; those three gouges were on the outside of the glass. He looked down, trying to find a way someone could have climbed up to the second storey and deliberately frightened her. There was nothing. No way anyone could have done that. Not without a ladder, and there was no ladder, no sign that any ladder had been in the garden.

"Jesus," he whispered. "Lord, what has happened here?"

He went back to the kitchen. "Okay, Bells, let's

put you in the guest room tonight. We'll deal with getting the glass replaced tomorrow."

Niccola reached across the table and took both her daughter's hands in hers. "Arabella, you need to tell us what you have been doing to bring this sort of attack on. I've seen some horrible stuff in my time, but never anything like this." She looked intently at the girl who was hanging her head, not meeting her mother's eyes.

"Bella?" Niccola let out a deep sigh.

Shoving her mother's hands away, Arabella allowed her fear to turn into anger. "Nothing. I haven't done anything," she lied. "Why do you always think everything is my fault! Leave me alone." Pushing her chair back, so that it screeched against the floor tiles, she ran out upstairs to her room. Grabbing her favourite pillow, she ran down the hallway to the guest room, slammed the door, and threw herself across the bed, where she cried herself to sleep.

In her cottage, Evelyn was pacing. "Lord, you brought me to this place. I don't understand how that newspaper thing happened, but there is no doubt you brought me here. But Father, this is getting really difficult. Bella seems to have made a decision to do everything that is contrary to your word, to completely destroy her own life. And Lord! She's only fifteen! Father, we need your help desperately."

Janel waited silently. She knew there was more going on than a teenager acting out. Everything on the earth had a spiritual counterpart.

While none of them was allowed to intervene except to save Arabella from any physical harm, they could, however, bring the heart of the Almighty to her parents and adopted Grandmother. They could and did encourage them to pray according to His will. Janel continued her stream of praise to God.

Evelyn caught the stream and rode it, her cries of anguish for Arabella changing and ascending as praise. Her words of truth reached the leaden ceiling of despair, which then started to crack. Evelyn stood in the middle of the room. She sensed the Angelic, which bolstered her faith. Continually pouring out her heart's love for the Creator brought fresh and renewed hope. Janel touched Evelyn's hand and put the written word of God into it.

Raising both her hands to her Lord, Evelyn spoke, her voice calling out into the Spirit realm, calling and demanding a response. Her faith soared, her voice reverberating throughout the earth, beyond space and into the very throne room of God.

In the corner of the bedroom where Arabella slept, a demon of torment from Discordia's lair sniggered. Oh, his mistress would be so full of praise for how he was fulfilling his mission.

Eliora glared at him. "You won't win. She has been blood-bought."

The tormentor snickered in arrogance. "Oh yes, we will. Look, she's already there. Look at her Bible. It's covered in dust. How long since she's opened it? Her parents won't be able to force her into their way of thinking for much longer nor keep control of her. No. You have lost." The demon, so assured of his victory, chortled in glee. "And look. Not long now until she allows death in. She has opened herself up and given us authority over her life," he snickered. "She might be sleeping in another room tonight, but that doesn't stop me! Where she goes, I go. She chose us, not you."

And that was a fact. But only partially true, for Hell cannot speak truth. Eliora would wait and continue her guard, her confidence in the Lord God unshakeable.

Arabella stirred in her sleep, her mouth muttering what she was dreaming.

There was a large lion. He stared at her with beautiful, soft amber eyes drawing her in. "Come ride with me, Arabella." The lion invited her closer until she found herself in the lion, her arms inside his front legs and her legs as his hind legs.

With a powerful thrust, the lion pushed off from the earth. Arabella could see through his eyes, hear with his ears and feel his might. Up, up, up. Still further up. Past the earth. Up. Past the moon. Higher. Further. Faster.

The lion stopped. Just stopped in the middle of the place where the stars sang. She looked out through his eyes at the stars and the planets— beautiful galaxies and constellations. With the lion's ears, she heard them all singing their praises to God. Their song was so beautiful, with no words, and yet she understood what they sang.

The lion stretched his paw out, and they were outside of time. Outside of time, outside of the physical dimension, they sat and watched the earth turn, seasons passing, and the stars, moon and sun all rode through their celestial orbits. They sat watching time pass by, revelling in the beauty of the lion's creation.

The lion spoke, "I miss you, my Arabella."

Back in her bed, tears leaked from Bella's eyes in her sleep.

The demon in her room flinched and cringed away at the presence of the lion.

In her cottage, Evelyn was unable to sleep. She sat in her favourite chair, staring out of the window at the dark night sky. Her thoughts were chaotic, tumbling around, over and over. She replayed again in her mind the last scene with Arabella.

Bella had come home from school. Evelyn had heard the front door slam and called out as she always did, "Hello, lovely girl." Arabella had screamed at her, "Don't you call me lovely girl!

You're not my grandmother. You have never been my grandmother. Leave me alone!"

Sobbing, Evelyn automatically went to the kitchen to make a cup of tea, her balm and thinking space. She put her head on the kitchen counter and cried. Loud, agonising cries. "Lord, help me. Jesus, help me! I don't think I can handle this any longer. Father! Help me!" She ripped off a paper towel to blow her nose on, made her tea, and carried it back to her chair.

Janel prayed for her, and in loving compassion, put her arms around the woman. "Lord God, show me what to do for this woman whom you have charged me with guarding." She prayed, her face beholding that of the Father. He spoke, and she nodded, singing His praise, her heart and mind filled with awe for the Lord. Back in Evelyn's lounge room, she nudged the older woman and said, *'Pick up the phone and call Angela and Christina. Get them to pray for Arabella.'*

"Lord," Evelyn prayed out loud. "Father, what has happened to Bella? I've been through teenage angst with my three children, but nothing like this. I don't understand. She is being tormented dreadfully." She put her head back and just stared at the ceiling. "Shall I call Angela and Christina and get them to intercede, as well? It's really late, Lord. Okay, they won't mind. Yes, I will."

It wasn't a hard decision to make. Her two best friends were also the best people she knew to storm Heaven, pray over bad situations, and see them change.

Janel smiled in satisfaction.

Angela and Christina came over immediately, still in their dressing gowns. As Christina said, "It's only 11:30, and who knows if any of us old girls will sleep tonight anyway."

Three women united, joining their voices as one, a threefold cord not easily broken. Angels filled the room. Warrior angels. Angels carrying scrolls of destiny. Angels of praise. Angels whose sole purpose was to do the Lord's will, enforcing His Kingdom on earth.

The atmosphere was thick with glory, unseen gems falling around the women bringing their truths: blood-red rubies of sacrifice; diamonds of purity, striking hammers, wisdom, zeal, the strength of God, that of abrasion bringing a time of reckoning, healing and deliverance; and carbuncle, whose meaning is a thundering arrowhead.

It was the divinely appointed time of deliverance for Arabella.

Evelyn stood shaking under the anointing of Holy Spirit, her voice calling into the kingdoms of principalities, thundering through eternity, striking as a flashing sword, rightly dividing the word of truth. "Lord," she cried loudly, her voice holding great authority. "You have given this child, Arabella, into my care. I was a widow, and you placed me in this family. Therefore, by the right given to me by Arabella's parents, in my authority and before all the realms there are, I call forth the books of Arabella's life. I speak out her destiny, as spoken over her before she left the Lord God Almighty's heart and came to this earth. I declare and decree that all will be fulfilled just as it is written. Jesus, I ask that you rebuke the powers of Hell and deal with this rebellion and destruction."

Time trembled, stretching into past, present and future. Wave after wave echoed through eternity, saturating Hell with the knowledge of failure. Glorifying Almighty God in His justice and righteousness. With Evelyn, Angela, Christina, Niccola and Joshua all praying, the Angels of the household knew that victory was imminent. They knew that God heard the fervent prayers of righteous people. They knew that praying people achieved a lot.

The three women sat in silence; the heaviness of glory speaking all that needed to be said.

CHAPTER NINETEEN

Niccola was doing her usual early morning rush, getting ready for work, trying to organise a recalcitrant teenager, and feeding the animals when her cell phone rang.

"Hi, Bronnie."

"How's Bella, Nic? I've been really worried about her. Why don't you send her to me for the school break?"

Niccola considered the idea. "That might work. Get her away from the group she's got involved in. I'll ask her. I have to rush now, Bronster." Niccola said, calling her sister by her childhood name. "I'll talk to Bella and get her to call you later, okay? Bye."

If it had been more than a few days until the school break, Arabella would have driven her parents crazy. She adored her Aunt Bronnie, and when the end of the school term came on Friday, Evelyn picked her up from school and put her on the plane to her Aunt's city.

Which then left Evelyn free for a much-needed week's break.

Early the following morning, Evelyn stirred in her sleep, the insistent noise of the phone demanding her attention. "Hello," she answered, her speech thick with sleep.

"Evelyn!" A voice chirruped down the phone. "Long time since we caught up. Put the coffee on."

Struggling to sound sensible in her half-asleep state, Evelyn answered, "Uh, Yes. It's a long story... Um, sorry, but who is this?" She struggled to wake up.

"It's Michelle. Don't you recognise the number?"

"Uh, sorry, I was asleep. Hang on." Evelyn rubbed her hands over her face and reached for her glasses. "OH! Michelle! What time is it? Michelle, it's only 7 am. Hey, Hang on. Where are you? What?" questions poured out of Evelyn faster than her sleep-fuddled brain could keep up with. "Hang on, let me wake up."

Michelle laughed, her gurgling giggle coming down the phone loudly, acting as a better alarm clock than the phone ringing.

Pushing the bedclothes off, Evelyn sat on the side of the bed. "Right. Now I feel sensible. Michelle, it's so wonderful to hear your voice. What time is it there?"

"Same time as you. I'm in the car outside. Open up. I need a coffee."

Evelyn stood up in shock. "You're here? When did you arrive? Why didn't you tell me you were coming?" The questions poured out fast.

"Just unlock the door and wave, so I can see where your cottage is." Michelle laughed and hung up.

Dragging her dressing gown on and scrambling to open the door to show Michelle where she was, Evelyn's head was whirling. Michelle's practicality and zest for adventure could be just what she needed at the moment. "Oh, Michelle!" Evelyn was caught into a ferocious hug from her friend. "I'm so confused. When did you get in?"

"Enough already, I need the toilet and then coffee, in that order, and then I'll tell all."

Evelyn put the kettle on to boil, setting out her trademark china cups and saucers, together with plates for toast, while Michelle wandered around looking through the cottage, outside to the private courtyard and back in, to grin at her friend.

"When I've had my first cup of coffee, then I'll talk. Ooh, and hot buttered toast with some of your divine preserves. Oh, I've missed those." She drank her coffee, holding the cup out for a refill. "Right. Well, it was a spur of the moment thing. I was dreaming of coming home for a visit one day, so was just googling my way through airfares when a special deal popped up. Mick said I may as well take it while it was cheap, and so I did, and here I am."

"Your Mick is a lovely man, isn't he?" Evelyn smiled. Her friend had found her love later in life, and he had been the epitome of God's saving the best things for last. "What do you have planned?"

"Well, I thought I would like to spend a few days with you. In fact, I'm hoping you can get some time off, and we can go away. I have always wanted to do the Tranz Alpine Railway Crossing, and as it's winter..." she stopped, leaving the unspoken question poised between them.

Evelyn's eyebrows shot up, her mouth falling open. "It just so happens I do have this week off. Bella is at her Aunt's for the week, and I'm free. It was always a dream of David's and mine to make that trip. I would love to go with you. Why don't we fly to Christchurch, spend two nights there, do the Tranz Alpine Crossing, stay two nights on the coast and then back home, so that will be four nights?"

Michelle punched Evelyn lightly on the shoulder. She giggled like a school girl let out on an adventure, then gave a yawn. "I'm tired. It was a long flight. Is it okay if I have a couple of hours' sleep while you organise the bookings?"

Their flight early the next morning marked the date stamp of freedom in Evelyn's life, the moment of leaving the grief of her widowhood behind, where she stepped into the joy of discovering life again.

For two lovely days, the women poked into corners of Christchurch, looked at the scars left by the earthquake, stared at the grief of the 185 names written on the memorial wall, and in awe looked at the demolished cathedral - the brutal results of the earthquake. They hired a rental car and drove out to the Akaroa Peninsula, exploring the early French stronghold of colonial times.

The following day, after an early start, they found their seats on the train.

"I'm so hungry," Michelle said. "No time for breakfast this morning. Do you think the dining car will be open yet?"

Like two schoolgirls, they giggled about anything at all. Their Angels laughed. The joy being released over the two women was contagious. As the train pulled away from Christchurch city, houses clustered together slowly grew further apart, then only an occasional farmhouse being seen in the middle of snow-covered, flat open country. The Waimakariri River appeared and disappeared as the train climbed to ascend the Southern Alps. At Arthur's Pass, the train stopped, and the passengers were allowed off for a short time. They stood on the snow-covered platform, looking at the remarkable scenery. Evelyn's eyes were filled with sudden tears, a dream long-held now fulfilled.

"Uh, excuse me," a young man tentatively touched Evelyn's shoulder.

She blinked as her reverie was broken and smiled at the young man.

"Um, this might sound strange, but I have a message for you from God." He was self-conscious, his cheeks pink with discomfiture. "Father God says to tell you that He is very proud of you. He knows and has heard your cry, and the answer has already been released." He looked at her as though ready to retreat, not knowing what to expect.

Evelyn's eyes closed, she let out a great sigh, and her head slumped forward.

Taking a deep breath, she opened her eyes again and reached out to take the man's hand. "This is not what I expected to find in Arthur's Pass, but then God knows where we are and all about us. Thank you. Your word has been delivered accurately. Thank you." She put her arms around the man and hugged him briefly. "I needed to hear that. Bless you, for your willingness to be thought a fool. Thank you."

'Father,' she whispered inside, *'Father you have heard. Thank you.'*

The rest of the rail trip did not disappoint, nor did their exploration of the West Coast. Standing at the Punakaiki Pancake Rocks, listening to the boom, boom, boom, of the ocean pounding through the blowholes, exclaiming at the magnificence of it all, Michelle said, "We had a guest speaker at church in Ireland. He was talking about the Mazzaroth. Have you ever heard of it, Evie?"

"Mazzaroth," Evelyn considered the word. "I don't think I have. What is it?"

"It's in the book of Job, where God is asking Job all the questions, like, where were you when I laid the foundation of the world. He preached about what the Mazzaroth means. I was just curious to know if you had heard of it, that's all," she shrugged.

As their adventures came to an end, Evelyn hugged her friend. "You have been such a God-sent blessing, Michelle. I can't thank you enough. And oh, I'm going to miss you so much when you go back to Ireland."

One final hug and Evelyn had to board her flight, leaving Michelle waiting for hers. Their paths, once again, leading down separate roads: Evelyn back to Arabella, and Michelle on to visit her family.

❧❧

Bronnie was enjoying her niece's visit. As she said, having a young person around woke her desire to look again and see life through the eyes of youth.

Shopping and junk food seemed a mandatory 'must do' on a teenager's list, and Bronnie revelled in it but frequently claimed to need coffee.

"Bella, I need coffee. Now. Please," she pleaded, her feet starting to ache and her caffeine fix long overdue. "C'mon. Let's sit in this café. Indulge your Aunt."

Once they were seated, Bronnie said, "Bella" She paused, unsure how to draw her niece out. "What happened? You were always so self-assured, and when I went to your baptism, you absolutely knew that you wanted to follow God forever. So what happened?"

Miserably, Arabella twisted a paper serviette in her hands, pulling at it until it ripped. She bit at her bottom lip.

Bronnie reached across the table and put her hand on her niece's hand.

"Tell me what happened, Love," she said softly, reluctantly pulling her hand away from Arabella as their drinks and food were brought to their table. Somehow, Aunt Bronnie was able to draw Arabella out, as her parents couldn't. She had never married and didn't have any children.

Idly, Arabella wondered if that was why she felt so close to her Aunt. Maybe her Aunt was still a teenager in her mind?

Arabella bit into her slice of ginger crunch, deliberately not looking at Bronnie. "Why do people have to be so mean!" she blurted out. "My friends at school and then those horrible people at church. I thought Christians were supposed to love you, be kind, you know, nice." Desperately, she tried to control the horrible snuffly crying.

Bronnie pushed her glass of water into Arabella's hand. "Here, have a drink. It will help you get control."

Arabella nodded and obediently gulped the water down. The action of drinking the water helped her gain control.

"Right Arabella, now tell me what happened. Start at the beginning and don't leave anything out."

It was a very long coffee break. Arabella told

her Aunt all that she had held inside for so long: the pain of rejection, then the betrayal of those at church who should have protected her. "Mrs Brown was so horrible, Aunt Bronnie. I would see her talking to her friends and pointing at me. And then their kids would start to mock me in youth group."

She talked about how she had felt so bad when she spoke to her parents and Evelyn rudely but couldn't seem to control it. The pain inflicted by those at church who should have protected her, turning to anger.

When she spoke about the games at Kilynn's birthday and the claw marks on the outside of the window, Bronnie finally understood.

"You haven't told your parents about these games, have you?" she said. "Because if you had, I know they would have seen the connection immediately. I think that when we get home, we should write it all down. Sometimes it's easier to 'talk' by writing it down, and then when you go home, you can give it to your parents to read." She looked carefully for her niece's reaction.

Looking every bit a miserable young teenager, Arabella nodded her yes, finally relinquishing the darkness inside.

Eliora glowed. She wept with joy and in awe of the way Holy Spirit works in all human lives. The Angels who were in the café with their precious people, gave a shout of praise to God, making the heavens ring with Hallelujah.

CHAPTER TWENTY

Niccola waited for Arabella's flight to arrive. She was excited to see her daughter, but also anxious, not knowing which Arabella was going to present first: the loving child she had always known or the snarling argumentative teenager.

"Mum!" Arabella came through the double doors into the waiting area. Niccola staggered under the full weight of her child, grabbing her in a ferocious hug. Hugging each other, they walked to the baggage collection area.

"Yay, you're home. It's been so quiet this week. Evelyn also went on vacation. Would you like to go to your favourite café on the way home?"

"Mm, nope. Thanks. I just want to get home and see Toby and Saffie. And my house and Dad and Grandma." She looked at her mother anxiously. "Did Dad fix my window? Is my bedroom safe again?"

"Yes. He got the glazier in and changed the glass. The marks are gone." She put her arm around her daughter's shoulder and hugged her tight. "It's safe again now, Love."

Just like a child, Arabella remarked on familiar landmarks as they drove home, finally giving a huge smile as they pulled into their garage. "Toby," she called as she pushed the car door open. "Toby, TOBY!" she called loudly. The little tripod heard and ran, barking his welcome, his crazy run wobbling as fast as he could towards the voice of his young mistress.

Niccola followed her daughter into the house, carrying the bag and lugging it up the stairs to her room. She could hear the 15-year-old charging around like a child, going from room to room as though she'd been away for months, not a week. 'Thank you, Lord, oh thank you, Father,' she whispered.

Arabella ran over to Evelyn's cottage, barging in without knocking. "Grandma. I'm home!" without giving Evelyn time to get out of her chair, Arabella crammed herself in beside her, resting her head on the older woman's shoulder.

'Father,' Evelyn silently prayed. *'Thank you. May this not just be an emotional response to being home, but the result we have been praying for.'*

"Come for dinner tonight, okay?" Arabella commanded. "I want to talk to all of us together." And like a whirlwind, she was off again. "See you later, Grandma."

Eliora sat on the bed with Arabella as the girl unpacked her case. She could see the light starting to glimmer through the dark armour Arabella had erected around herself.

Arabella's fingers hovered over folded sheets of paper. She bit her top lip and put the papers aside onto her pillows, continuing to put her clothes away until the case was empty. Picking the sheets of paper up, she continued to sit, holding them. Contemplative.

Eliora bowed her head, praying for courage for the girl.

Arabella stood and took the pieces of paper into her mother's office, where she printed off three copies.

It was dinner time. Josh had come home from work. Evelyn came to the main house to help prepare the meal.

Four people sat around the table. Josh gave thanks. "Father God, how I thank you for the safe return of our daughter, for the love and joy she brings to us all. And Lord, we thank you for your provision to us always. Amen."

Arabella remained silent throughout the meal. Evelyn watched her, praying quietly in her heart, wondering what was coming.

Giving a large sigh, Arabella pushed her empty plate away, and took the copied pieces of paper from her lap. Not speaking, she put a copy in front of each person. Her mother looked at her speculatively.

"Um. Aunt Bronnie helped me write this. I want you to read it all. Please don't ask me any questions. Just read it."

"Okay, Honey," her father said as he started to

read what she had written.

Niccola gave an agonised cry as she realised the root cause of her daughter's misbehaviour over the last year. How could she have missed the signs? Why wasn't she there for her? She stifled noisy sobs of pain.

Wiping his eyes as surreptitiously as he could, Josh said nothing, laying the documents on the table, waiting for the others to finish.

Arabella sat there, wiping her eyes, blowing her nose as the emotions breached her hardened heart.

"Oh my goodness," was all Evelyn said, reaching over to hold Arabella's hand.

The family's Angels also stood silently. They knew what had been written. They also knew the great evil it unveiled, and if there was one thing the enemy hated, it was to be exposed.

Josh cleared his throat, trying to find a way to open the conversation, a way that wouldn't shut his daughter down again.

Eliora spread her wings, covering her charge in love.

Zarad walked through the wall, the glory on him lighting the room up. Arioch followed him, his sword held directly at the demon, which followed Arabella everywhere she went. "You are on borrowed time," he informed the demon.

The demon shuddered and shrieked, hiding his eyes.

"Do you want to talk about this, Arabella?" her father spoke quietly.

She nodded, the words jammed in her throat. She desperately wanted someone to pull the words out of her, to ask the right question so that she could explain.

Evelyn understood. "It was the disappointment of being betrayed, first by the mean girls at school and then with Keagan and his mother and all her friends, wasn't it, Bella?"

She nodded. "It wasn't fair. I didn't do anything. And then suddenly, no one liked me anymore. I thought that if people went to church, they must love Jesus too, but they were horrible. Lauren tried to help me. I've been so lonely." As the sobs of such painful rejection broke, so did the dam. And from there, the entire story unfolded. She left nothing out. Not the anger, nor the bewilderment, and not the evil door she had unlocked to allow darkness in to torment her.

"Please, I want to be alone now," she said. "I just need some time to think about this."

No one tried to stop her as she left the table and went upstairs to her room, shutting the door behind her.

Sniffling, Arabella reached for a tissue from her bedside table. At that moment, Eliora moved over to stand right by the table and manifested the radiance of God so that she shone brilliantly. The reflection lit up the Bible on the bedside table so that it looked as though the sun's rays illuminated the book.

Bella hesitated as she pulled the tissue from the box. It had been months; no, probably more like a year since she had opened her once precious Bible. Slowly, hesitantly, nearly reluctantly, but compelled to, she moved to pick the book up, almost shy about opening what had once been her constant companion. She sat up and stroked the cover.

Eliora held her breath.

Arabella touched the cover, her forefinger slowly moving across from top to bottom, feeling the embossed lettering in the soft suede, coming back to trace the indented cross.

She picked it up, almost afraid. It felt so right, so familiar and loved.

The Bible seemed to fall open of its own volition. Eliora quickly flipped the pages to 1 John. The radiance being illuminated through Eliora highlighted chapter one, verse nine.

Bella's eyes looked at where the light fell. She read the verse quietly to herself. "If we confess our sins, He is faithful and just and will forgive us our sins and purify us from all unrighteousness." Plop. A single tear fell on the page. Plop. Plop. Plop. Tears were streaming down her face. Suddenly, she saw. "Jesus. I'm so sorry. Lord, Forgive me." She saw all the filth, the evil. Everything that had drawn her away from Truth and into lies. The past year spent in anger and deceit. A life of hatred, drawing her down into the very belly of Hell. All her rebellion was laid bare.

A radiance lit the room. Eliora bowed low.

Jesus sat on the bed next to Arabella. "Satan desired to sift you, Arabella, but I prayed that once the sifting was over, that your faith would not fail. I forgive you, my beloved. I have so missed you. Come, let's dance together as we used to. You have much, much more to learn, my little lioness."

Arabella looked up, her face suffused with joy. The dreadful hatred that had lingered around, stifling life and freedom, had gone, replaced with that love she had always known. "I missed you, Jesus. I missed you so much. I'm so sorry."

Eliora fell to her knees in adoration. "Lord God. Thank you!"

CHAPTER TWENTY-ONE

As Arabella slept that night, her eyes moved restlessly, reflecting her dream state.

"Arabella," the lion called her, His voice a wisp in her dreams. Her eyelids flickered as she listened to the lion.

"Arabella," the lion spoke softly now.

She could hear Him calling to her, but the forest was so thick that she couldn't see a path to get to where she could hear Him.

"Where are you?" she called. "I can't find you."

"Look in your heart. Follow my voice. My sheep know my voice."

She stopped picking her way through the scrub and undergrowth and stood still, listening.

"Follow my voice. My sheep know my voice."

She knew that voice. Follow my voice, He said. She started walking again, and as she concentrated on listening to the voice, the path became clearer, wider, opening up before her.

She noticed the trees were thinning out, could hear the sound of water, a stream running, and see the sunlight ahead. Carefully, she made her way from the darkness of the forest towards the grassy area she could see ahead. The Lion continued to call her.

"Arabella, my Beloved, come to me."

Her legs brushed past the ferns, and she finally stepped out of the dimness into the sunlight, her bare feet cushioned on the soft grass.

And she saw Him.

He turned around, and as He held his hand out to her, she saw it was Jesus. She walked towards Him. Towards the sound of the living water, towards the light, and put her hand into His. She sat on the soft grass next to Him.

He looked at her. "I have missed you, my Arabella," He said, as He kissed her forehead.

She lay down with her head on his lap and fell asleep.

The sun woke her as it peeked into her bedroom. She yawned and stretched, surprised to find herself in bed, in her room, and not with the Lion. "I missed you too, Jesus," she whispered to Him.

Saturday. Her first day back home. Saturdays were family days. Niccola would often take Arabella shopping, and as a family, they would do something in the afternoon. But this Saturday, Joshua was on call, and Niccola had a trade fair. Arabella slept late, wandering downstairs well after her usual wake-up time, only to find the house deserted. There was a note on the kitchen counter.

ARABELLA

'Been called out to work. Grandma is at home. Love you, Dad'

Yawning and stretching, Arabella opened the fridge, peered inside, and shut it again. Nothing instant in there. Still in her nightclothes, she wandered outside, and Toby scuttled up to her in his tripod way, wagging his tail and whining the loving *'so pleased you are here, I haven't seen you forever'* moan the funny little dog gave his people.

"Come on, Tobester, let's go to Grandma's and see if she's got anything decent for breakfast. I'll race you." Laughing, Arabella, with the dog chasing her, ran across the lawn to Evelyn's cottage.

"Grandma! It's me. Mum and Dad are out."

Evelyn looked up from reading her Bible as Arabella pranced in the back door. "Hello, lovely girl. Did you sleep well? You must have; it's nearly 10 o'clock."

"Have you got anything to eat? There's nothing at our house." Arabella looked hopefully at Evelyn.

"You mean, please, Grandma, would you cook me something because I know full well that your fridge and pantry are full," Evelyn laughed as she got up and started opening the fridge, pulling out some eggs and a pan from the cupboard. "Omelette or scrambled eggs?"

"Omelette, please," Arabella settled herself on the kitchen barstool, watching Evelyn cook, and fiddling with stuff on the kitchen counter.

"Grandma," the fiddling stopped.

"Mmm?"

Clearing her throat, Arabella tried again. "Grandma, I talked with Jesus last night. I told Him how sorry I was for all this, this..." her voice trailed off, not sure what to call the past year; a hand indicating that which was in the past. "Well, you know how I've been. Anyway, so I talked to Him. But with all I've learned, I keep feeling there are tendrils, you know, like an octopus, that are still trailing after me. How do I get rid of them?"

Evelyn stopped whisking the eggs. "Yes, dear, you did open some gates that were never meant to be opened, which is why God tells us very clearly in the Bible not to do these things. They only lead us to destruction."

Arabella fidgeted with the salt and pepper shakers on the kitchen bench.

When the omelette was cooked, Evelyn handed Arabella the plate with her breakfast on it. "Hot chocolate?" Evelyn asked. "And then, would you like to cut off those tendrils that are still attached to you? To close off the doors you opened into the demonic kingdom?" Two questions: one needing an immediate answer, the other for which she was content to wait a while.

"Yes, please," she cut a hole in her omelette, then another, and then a curvy hole. She grinned. "Smiley face omelette," she said, before looking very serious. "I can't go back to how I was. I need to lock that door, and I can't go back to doing what

I used to do." Pausing only long enough to eat her omelette, she finally put her fork down.

"Grandma, I'm finding it really hard. If I don't do the same things with my friends, then they won't want to be friends anymore, and I don't have any other friends." She looked up at Evelyn, her eyes slowly filling with tears.

Evelyn sighed. The seeming enormity of a teenager's world and their limited experience of life skewed the view, leaving them unable to see clearly. Everything was a major issue. Life began and ended with acceptance by their friends.

"Let's just deal with the immediate issue of the open doors and gates, shall we? And then we'll pray and ask the Lord to bring you a new group of friends."

The demons and evil spirits who had attached themselves to Arabella, looked alarmed. They started frantically to call for Trivia to help. Her dominion was thrown into immediate chaos. Their prize was about to be snatched away.

"Resist, resist as hard as you can. Remind that brat of your legal right to be there. Do not give in," she yelled at them, while astral travelling to Discordia's principality.

"It's your fault," she screeched. "This is your assignment, and you are legally liable to deliver to his majesty the results he has demanded. Don't you dare try to put the blame on me when we are summoned."

Discordia was stunned. She had been so sure that the plan would work, But HE had interfered, just as He had In The Beginning. "I hate Him. I hate Him," she threw herself around in a red rage, kicking, ripping and shredding anything and any of her underlings that got in her path. "Don't let her order you to go," she screamed at the demons hanging onto Arabella. "Stay there, embed yourselves. Hide. Do anything except leave."

In Evelyn's kitchen, Arabella shuddered, icy fingers clasping tighter, around her neck, in her mind, desperately trying to find any place to hide.

Eliora radiated light, its frequency setting up vibrations within the spirit realms. More Angels joined her, singing their praises to the great Deliverer.

"Arabella, you must now openly repent of allowing these horrible things into your life. I know you have done it privately, but there is power in confessing before others. Then you need to renounce, which means to recant, to break covenant with the evil you have opened yourself up to."

The girl looked at Evelyn with eyes that pleaded for help.

Tentatively, Arabella started to speak. "God, I repent for doing all these things that I knew you didn't want me to do. I did it willfully and knowing that it was wrong. I ask that the Blood of Jesus wash me clean from my sin and that you would hold out your sceptre of forgiveness over me."

Evelyn nodded. "Carry on, Love."

The evil spirits started choking and wailing.

"Jesus, I ask that you cover me under your blood. I repent for having allowed myself to enter into the dark realms by playing those games. I renounce utterly any and all hold the filth of Hell has placed over me. I now break with the covenant I made with evil and ask that you deliver me, Jesus."

The light of Heaven started to vibrate at a higher frequency shattering the lethal cords of Hell over Arabella.

The demons dug deeper into her. They clung tightly, trying to find any vestige of legal right to stay where they were.

Arabella started coughing. Evelyn calmly called on the name of Yeshua. She had seen this many times before.

"Bella," she said. "Tell them to leave in the name of Yeshua. The name Jesus is a more recent English translation; His name in Hebrew is Yeshua."

"In the name of Yeshua, who is the Christ, He who is God, I command these demons to leave me now." With that, the fight for freedom was won.

The demons were forcibly ejected from their comfortable home. Their battle was lost.

Arabella slumped over the kitchen counter, exhausted. She felt clean, fresh, and as Eliora touched her, the life of Jesus started to flow through her DNA, reviving and refreshing her spirit.

Yeshua stood by her and breathed new life into Arabella's spirit. A fresh start. He glared at the demons who dared to stay. They fled howling, through the realm of time and into their lost eternity.

"Well done, Eliora," the Lord told the Angel. "Very well done, indeed." He turned to Evelyn and put His hand on her head. "This one is strong. She has endured much. The pain she has been through has created a place of love in her life, and because she did not allow bitterness to enter, I am able to express my love through her. Well done, my treasured daughter."

The presence of the Lord rested on Evelyn. The heavy weight of His glory encompassed her, and she staggered to her chair.

"Thank you, Yeshua. Oh, Thank you, Yeshua," was all Evelyn could say.

She opened her eyes to see Arabella kneeling by her. "Thank you, Grandma. Thank you for praying for me and for loving me. They've gone now. I can feel those tendrils have gone. I feel clean again."

Evelyn patted her hand. "I love you, Arabella. You truly are so very precious."

After Arabella left, Evelyn sat in her customary chair. All she could say was, "Thank you, Lord." It had been a difficult season, but as always, Father God was faithful.

Evelyn's cell phone rang. She picked it up, smiling as she recognised the number. "Michelle, my adventurous friend. Are we off on another trip?" she laughingly said by way of greeting.

"Oh, I wish! No, I just called to catch up. How was the teenage climate when you got home?" Michelle's query referenced the angry Arabella.

Evelyn smiled broadly. "You will never guess what happened when she got home. The Lord is magnificent." Evelyn took the phone with her to the kitchen, chatting while making herself some tea.

All in all, Janel reflected, as she listened to Evelyn telling Michelle about Arabella's turn-around, the Lord is so faithful, so good to His children. *And I*, she thought, *am so privileged to be part of His grand design.*

SPIRIT WALKER

ARABELLA

MY DAUGHTER, CHILD OF MY HEART

CHAPTER TWENTY-TWO

Jesus placed a picture in front of Arabella. It was Mrs Brown. Arabella's heart knocked sideways, just a little.

"I want you to forgive her, Arabella," He said as He laid more and more pictures on the table. "And forgive all these people, as well." The weight of his statement lay heavily.

She looked at the images, not really wanting to see the people represented by them. Her stomach tried to leave through her mouth, rebelling at what Jesus was asking her to do.

She looked at Jesus. He smiled at her.

"If you won't forgive others, then my Father won't be able to forgive you. But there's more to it than that. As you forgive others, then you release the bitterness that is growing inside you." Jesus looked at her seriously, "If you allow that bitterness to grow, then the light you carry now, will gradually be extinguished. You will no longer be a light bearer."

Arabella put a finger on the picture of Mrs Brown, the woman who had caused her so much pain with her gossiping and self-righteousness. "How can I do that? Every time I think of her, it squeezes my insides."

"Exactly. That is literally eating you alive. This is why forgiveness is so important. But there's more to forgiveness than just this. As you forgive those who hurt you, it not only releases you from pain, it opens the way for their healing as well."

She considered what He said. "Okay, I understand that. But how do I forgive them? If I simply say 'I forgive Mrs Brown,' it's not truly forgiving, is it? Because it keeps coming back."

"That is where you need my faith," Jesus told her. "Take my hand and forgive all these people, all the mean girls, all the gossipy women, forgive Keagan. As you are willing to forgive them, I will give you my faith to add to yours. Shall we try it?"

She nodded. "Jesus, I want to forgive these people for the pain they caused me." She reached out and took hold of His hand. "Jesus, I need your help to forgive because I can't forgive them by myself."

He beamed at her; He was thrilled that she obeyed so quickly. Inside Arabella's mind, a tendril of bitterness started to let go its hold on her.

"Now, let's look again. Have a look at what happened when you did that." He showed her through the spirit realm what she had done. Tangles were starting to unfurl; light was beginning to glimmer in dark places.

He clapped His hands in delight. "I want to show you something else now. I want you now to release a blessing over Mrs Brown. Simply say, 'Father, I bless Mrs Brown,' and then watch what happens. But you must mean it, Arabella. It's not a trick you can play on God. He knows if you mean it or not."

"What, you mean ask God to bless her? Just say 'bless' without saying what sort of blessing?"

"Yes, because doesn't He always know what each person needs?"

Arabella laughed. "Yes, of course, He is God."

Jesus nodded His encouragement.

Bella took a deep breath. "Father God, I forgive Mrs Brown, and I ask you to bless her. I confess that I have allowed the enemy to use her to oppress me and bring an atmosphere of heaviness."

"Oh, that is wonderful, my Bella. Now watch."

They sat together and looked as shimmering light shot out from Heaven, touching Mrs Brown, instantly shooting the spark of life into her heart.

"Keep watching," Jesus instructed her.

The harshness on Mrs Brown's face softened. Just a little, but her heart had definitely been stirred.

"You see?" Jesus said. "This is the power of forgiveness and blessing. Just as I paid the greatest price to forgive you, so I ask you to forgive others, and as you do, you set in motion all of Heaven to work for both you and the person you are forgiving. But there is much more. Did you realise that you have the power to forgive others' sins? My beloved friend John wrote in his book, chapter 20 verse 23, 'If you forgive anyone his sins, they are forgiven; if you withhold forgiveness from anyone, it is withheld.' That is truly remarkable. But when you look at it from the aspect of Heaven, it all makes sense. If you are in me, and I am in you, then together, we forgive others. And as we forgive them, so Heaven forgives them as well."

Arabella shook her head. She had never heard this before. And yet she must have because she had read John's book many times. Maybe it was because Jesus was explaining it to her.

"It is written that I am the light of the world. Think about this, Bella; whatever frequency you view light at is what you see. So, I have shown you more light, and now you see more light. You are viewing things now from a higher frequency." He hugged her and blew on her. "Sleep now, precious Arabella. We will talk again."

The lingering memory of her night's encounter with Jesus brought with it understanding and mercy. While sitting alone during the lunch break, she saw Jerrah walking past, and this time, Arabella understood. "Lord, she's acting like that because she's hurting. Father, I forgive Jerrah for her nastiness, and I bless her. Father, I bless her right into the Kingdom."

The Angel assigned to Jerrah caught Arabella's blessing and poured it over the girl, watching as it seeped into her mind and ran down into her heart.

Sophie followed after Jerrah but looked at Arabella sitting alone. Her face pleaded with her.

Of all the pain the mean girls had inflicted, it was Sophie's betrayal that had hurt the most, for she had been a special friend for Bella. Yes, she was needy, but she had been someone to laugh with and share school break times. Now, Arabella saw her differently. "Father, look at Sophie. She is trapped in a web of her own making. I think she wants to get free but doesn't know how." A thought drifted across her mind.

Eliora smiled. Oh yes, her young charge was starting to understand.

"Sophie," Arabella called. "Come and sit with me."

The girl hesitated, glancing at Jerrah for her reaction. When Jerrah just shrugged disdainfully, she made her decision. She sat down next to Arabella.

"It's nice to talk with you, Bella," she said. "I'm sorry I've been so awful."

Arabella smiled, gratitude in her heart pouring out to Jesus for revealing another amazing truth.

"It's okay, Sophie. I understand now. Jesus taught me something amazing. Do you want to hear it?"

৩৫

Evelyn was glorifying the Lord, thanking Him for Arabella's freedom. She felt the presence of Angels near. Janel smiled. She was always near. After all, Evelyn was her special assignment. And now, she had a message for Evelyn. She placed in her hand a gem of an idea: *'Get a copy of the book of Enoch. Read the book of Job again. Find out about the Mazzaroth.'*

"Oooh," she said out loud; the Mazzaroth thought triggering another. "Michelle will be leaving for Ireland soon." She gave a very satisfied sigh. "Father, thank you for that time out with Michelle. I thoroughly enjoyed it. Thank you."

CHAPTER TWENTY-THREE

Jesus waited for Arabella to join him. He had chosen the beautiful Pleiades for their meeting. It was a strategic and important location. As He waited, He talked with the Seven Sisters of the Pleiades constellation, and they sang to him, their stellar harmonies interweaving with each other, just as they had for eons past.

It was time. "Arabella, come to me, Beloved."

Arabella stirred in her sleep, her spirit immediately alert. Listening to His voice as He called, knowing where to find Him. And she soared directly to the hot blue luminous cluster of stars. The Seven Sisters bowed to the King and continued their singing. Arabella stood in the night sky next to her Lord. Oh, how she loved Him. Everything in her longed never to leave again.

Against the singing stars, the glory of the marvellous creation, galaxies, constellations, nebulae. Such indescribable beauty. They sat in the middle of the Orion constellation quietly, both enjoying being with the other.

"Consider my Mazzaroth, Bella. I am going to redeem my Mazzaroth. That which was stolen and used for evil."

She looked at Him. "Your what? What's a Mazzaroth?"

Jesus laughed. "Most of mankind have no knowledge of the Mazzaroth, and yet it is clearly written," He said, waving His hand at the myriad of stars around them, "It is written in both the Word and in the heavens. But evil has taken my beautiful Mazzaroth and chained it in darkness, using its power for their own ends. And that end is to ensnare man. Call it back, Arabella. Call it by my Name, and I will redeem my Mazzaroth."

Arabella looked mystified.

"I know the number of stars. I have called them all by name. I made seasons to govern the years; the sun and the moon are the great luminaries, one for the night and one for the day. The Heavens declare my glory and righteousness, and when you look up to the sky and see the sun, the moon and the stars, all the heavenly array, do not be enticed into bowing down and worshipping them. This is what the evil nameless one has done, Arabella. He has coerced mankind and taught them to believe a shadow of my truth."

"Your Mazzaroth?" she asked.

He nodded. "Yes, my Mazzaroth. You see, my daughter, what I call my Mazzaroth, has been altered, oh, just a little bit, and with another little bit, until its original intent is no longer seen. Now, man calls it the Zodiac. They use it to foretell the future and call it astrology. It has bound all my creation into the occult."

Arabella's eyes were wide with sudden understanding. "Tell me more."

"I was hoping you would ask me that," He said. "My friend Enoch knew all about the Mazzaroth. He wrote it down so people would understand. But many centuries later, man decided that his writings were not important enough to be included in what is now called the Bible. But oh, it is so important, my Arabella. Enoch understood about the seasons, how the head of the seasons governed the times." He stopped speaking, looking out into the deepest blue of the heavens, where the stars seemed to twinkle and shine.

Arabella listened to the singing of the stars, humming a little with them. "Why can't I hear the stars during the day? Why do I have to wait till I'm with you?" she asked.

"One day, Beloved, all of mankind will be able to hear them. Sin will no longer have a hold over my creation. One day, everything will be made new."

She sighed, the sound one of great contentment. "I can't wait for then."

"No," He said. "I can't wait until then, either. How I long for my creation and my loved ones."

"The Mazzaroth was set as a sign for all of mankind to interpret what was coming, and so they would know about me. It was literally the 'gospel in the stars.' We put it there so that man would be looking for my coming and then understand."

Arabella looked doubtful. "How can some random stars tell all about you?" It's not like you put signs up here."

Laughing, Jesus acknowledged the truth of that. "Yes, you are right there, but what happened, by accident, of course," He rolled His eyes and laughed, "is that the patriarchs, Adam, Seth and Enoch, looked at the sky and saw the stars we had placed there. As Holy Spirit showed them how the various constellations belonged together, they wrote it down. It is all there if anyone cares to look.

"For example. The goat of Capricorn represents me as the scapegoat for sin. The sign Virgo represents the virgin birth, and Leo shows me as the Lion of Judah."

Bella's forehead wrinkled as she tried to understand what He was saying. "Therefore," she said, "people have taken that which was originally intended as prophesy and to mark the era the world was in, and made it all about themselves? They have actually made it rather small, haven't they? Very small. Hmm."

"Yes, they have. Let me explain just a little more. The twelve signs are arranged in three sets of four, each having its own subject in the grand plan of history. One to four shows the seed of the woman, representing me and what I would do. Five to eight, show the formation, career and destiny of my church. And nine to twelve is the great judgment period and the completion of the whole mystery of God concerning the world and man. Thus, nine being Taurus the bull, speaks of judgment, followed by the 'twins', who are the second Adam and Eve, representing the union of the church. The Scarab beetle is transformation, and Leo is the consummated victory. But that is enough for now, my Arabella. You will learn more as you go through your life. Remember, I will always be with you."

Arabella rolled over in her sleep, the memory of the encounter already fading but caught in her spirit, where it remained until it was needed.

After school the next day, Arabella skipped, jumped, and then remembering she was a teenager, walked as nonchalantly as she could to the house, hoping none of the other kids on the school bus had noticed. Until she got inside.

"Grandma," she yelled, dumping her bag by the front door and running into the kitchen. "Grandma, have you ever heard about something called Mazzaroth?"

"Milk and cookies, Love?" Evelyn seemed to ignore her question, getting the afternoon tea, and only when she was ready, complete with her cup of tea, did she answer Arabella's question.

"Actually, I do know something about the Mazzaroth. I've been reading about it for the last month. Why do you ask? I wouldn't have thought it would be something you knew about."

Nibbling around the outside of her cookie before responding, Arabella took her time, just as Evelyn had.

"Grandma, I had this really strange dream last night. Jesus told me He was going to restore His Mazzaroth. What do you think that means?"

Evelyn just stood in the kitchen, both hands over her mouth, her eyes large, filling with tears.

"Oh, Bella, is that what He said? Are you sure that's what He said?"

"Yes. Absolutely sure. He explained it to me a little bit, but I can't remember much about it." She looked at her grandmother. "Grandma, are you ok? Why are you crying?"

"Oh, Bella. Bella. This is huge," she choked back the emotion. "It means, beloved child, that He is restoring all things back to Eden. That's what that means."

CHAPTER TWENTY-FOUR

The Angels strode through the wildflower meadow, delightedly listening to the grasses and flowers singing praises. One would sing a few notes, to which the trees responded as they clapped their hands.

An Angel started singing, "Sound the trumpet in Zion, for the King is coming in."

"Worthy is the King, who reigns forever," another sang, and the notes skipped all through the meadow until it was buzzing with dancing joy.

The notes interwove and harmonised with each other, some playfully alighting on an Angel, then off flying again to create their own melodies. The Lights from Zion played in a shimmering myriad of colours, just as they had been created on earth, where heaven cups the world in a rounded curve, like a vaulted cathedral.

Jesus sat on the bough of a large tree on the edge of the meadow, watching these beautiful ones playfully make their way to Him. His longing for all creation to join Him was intense, and He and His Father had been working hard to draw all of mankind into the great heart of God.

Smiling at the Angels, He jumped out of the tree so that He could walk among them.

"There is still a lot to do." Jesus paced as He spoke. "Arabella has a long way to go before she is mature enough to work without constant instruction. Until she has grown enough, we have to continue to give her step-by-step guidance, gradually leaving out smaller pieces of information so that she is forced to seek it for herself and thus grow to maturity. If we continually give children instructions on how to do even the smallest task, they will never grow up. Therefore, the plan is to start training her in the path she needs to walk, teaching her who she is and how to wield her sword and my Word."

The Angels cheered loudly, agreeing with the Lord.

"Now that she is well-grounded in love, plans are being put into motion, so she will know who she is and start to understand the mysteries of Heaven. I am going to start to teach her how to co-create with me."

The murmur of approval grew.

"I will then move on to giving her a strong foundation in the knowledge of her authority."

Eliora nodded. *Yes,* she thought, *that is a good plan.*

Niccola and Arabella went to the mall on Saturday morning. "I need coffee," Niccola said, walking in the direction of her favourite in-mall cafe.

Arabella walked silently alongside. Her mind was occupied with the girl she had seen. For some reason, her attention had been drawn to her, compassion stirred, and she found herself praying for the girl.

"You get a table, Bells, and I'll order our drinks," Niccola directed.

As Arabella sat down, she continued her unspoken prayer vigil. She sought for guidance, *'Lord, how do you want me to pray for that girl?'* The answer was almost instant.

"How would you like to pray for her?"

Eliora smiled. The training had begun.

'Lord, I want to pray according to your will. What do you want me to pray?' The silent prayer from Arabella's heart was so beautiful to Jesus.

Again He answered her, "What would you like to pray for her?"

Confused, Arabella sat, unable to answer for a moment. *'But Lord, I want to pray what you want me to pray.'*

Jesus' reply was instant. This was the moment He had been waiting for. "Oh Arabella," Jesus chuckled, "Do you not yet know my heart? How much time have you spent getting to know me? You can pray whatever you want to for her. I know your heart, and I know that you will pray according to my heart. Whatever you pray, I will agree with."

Arabella was perplexed. This was outside of anything she had ever known. She hadn't known she could pray without receiving specific instructions, and that Jesus would agree with her. This was new. Tentatively she tried it. *"Lord, I pray that you will arrange that the girl will come to know you and that she will be brought into your Kingdom, Jesus."*

"AMEN!" Jesus said.

The Angels in the cafe all laughed and agreed with Him. The atmosphere in the cafe grew lighter, the people visibly relaxed as the spirit of love settled over them.

It was seldom that a believer grew mature enough to be taken through this process, and they loved it. Eliora was so proud of Arabella, and she was honoured to have been given this assignment.

"Good," Jesus said to Eliora. "Very good. Now let's extend the boundaries further. I need you to call her attention to an event that she will pass by on the school bus on Monday afternoon. The training will continue."

Eliora bowed before her Lord.

On Monday afternoon, Arabella stared out of the school bus window, her mind half on all the homework she had to do.

Eliora was watching, ready to nudge Arabella, to show her what Jesus wanted her to see. There it was.

Arabella looked at the crime scene tape around the gas station. *Horrible,* she thought, *they must have been robbed.* Her first instinct was to pray. *Lord, why do people have to do that! But I ask that no one was hurt in the incident.* Her wordless prayer was heard.

Jesus nodded at Justice. Justice whispered to Arabella, *'Where is the justice in this incident? What can be done about it?'*

The response welled up in Arabella. "Lord, where is the justice in this? Why is there so much crime and corruption?"

Jesus clapped His hands joyfully. This was going exactly as He wanted it to. He waited until Arabella got off the bus before speaking again. "What if you could pray for justice and righteousness?" He said to her, "And have Heaven legislate and agree with you?"

༺༻

"Grandma, I'm home," Arabella opened the door to the house and called out as she usually did.

"Hello, lovely girl," the response came from the kitchen.

Arabella dropped her bag by her seat in the kitchen and took a bite of the food Evelyn had prepared for her. "Mmm, nice cookies," Arabella mumbled through a mouthful of chocolate chip cookie. "Grandma, what does 'legislate' mean?"

"Legislate means to pass a law, to enforce something. Are you studying it at school?"

"No, not at school. Just wondering, that's all. I'd better go and do my homework. I've got masses of it." She picked up her school bag and went to her bedroom, pulling her books out of her bag and putting them on her desk.

"What do you mean by that, Jesus? Isn't everything on earth ruled by Heaven, anyway?" She chewed the end of her pen while her mind deliberated on what Jesus had said in the cafe the other week, and then today while she was coming home.

She pushed the conversation from her mind, turning her concentration instead to her homework.

While Arabella slept that night, Jesus called her. She met him in what looked like a half-moon shaped stadium, with a centre stage, so all could see what was happening. Looking around, she could see other people watching the proceedings. They seemed to be from the Earth, not Heaven.

"What is this place?" she asked.

"This is the Council of the Nations. It is where those of my government of man and Angels debate over the direction of their appointed countries, and the thoughts and intents of my Father and I are legislated into law. From there, the Angels take the law to ensure that it is enacted. This is what I wanted you to see; what I was telling you earlier today. As you pray for Justice and Righteousness, your prayers are brought here, debated, and together with the Twenty-Four Elders, are brought into law and thus from Heaven to Earth."

Arabella's thoughts tumbled frantically through her mind. "You mean that I can legislate your will into law, and the Angels ensure it is carried out?"

"That is precisely what I mean. But there is more to it than that. What you have just said is only the beginning. Do you remember the girl in the shopping mall?"

She nodded. "Yes, I remember. It was weird like I was able to tell you what to do."

He laughed. "I suppose it does seem like that. But this is what it means. When you pray according to my will, and it's easy to know what my will is, it's written in the Bible, and it's written in your heart, then as you pray, I co-create with you to ensure that what you have asked me for, happens."

She stared at Him. "Co-create?"

"I know it is outside of everything you have been taught, but if you read the creation story carefully, you will see that it is there, quite clearly. Adam was given the task of naming all the animals. That was co-creating with me. And in the gospels, I am in you, and you are in me. Anything you ask in my name, I will do it. You see, Arabella, the vast majority of my church are still babies. They are still very immature and keep asking me to do things instead of growing up and taking their authority to enforce my Kingdom on Earth. This is called the 'orphan' mind. Where my people do not know who they are. They keep referring to themselves as my servants. Long, long ago, I said, 'I no longer call you servants; I call you friends.' My heart has longed for true fellowship with those who love me. Those with whom I can entrust my Kingdom to."

He waved his hand at the venue, indicating the busy activity as the Angels debated, and then presented documents to the Twenty-Four Elders for swearing into law.

"This is where those who have attained maturity bring their decrees to sworn into law and then enforced on Earth. What I want you to learn, Arabella, is to co-create with me."

He took Arabella's hand, and immediately, they were in a different place, hovering over a church. People were all yelling 'in Jesus' name, in Jesus' name,' and as they did, they were waving toy wooden swords.

"What are they doing!" she exclaimed.

"These are my people who do not know who they are. They are little more than children all yelling my name, thinking it will invoke Heaven to act on their behalf. Because they are as children, I do answer them. I love them. But, for so long, they have been praying from Earth to Heaven, instead of taking their seats next to me, being seated with me in Heavenly places, and using their authority. Instead, they beg me. They do not realise who they are." He sighed. "If they did, they would legislate Righteousness and Justice, and it would be passed into law."

He turned to Arabella. "Come, you have seen enough for tonight. It's time to go."

ARABELLA

Arabella tossed in her sleep. Saffie sat up and glared at Eliora.

'Ssh, Saffie. Go back to sleep now, little cat,' Eliora stroked the cat's head.

CHAPTER TWENTY-FIVE

A new confidence enveloped Arabella. At Youth Group, she spoke with authority and, in church services, she found herself seeing far more behind what was being said. She smiled as her spirit saw the Angels in the church, and each time, her memory was triggered, remembering just a little more of her night-time encounters with Jesus. Somehow, what the other girls at school were doing, seemed of little interest. She had developed a new habit of excusing herself after dinner, to go to her room, where she would talk with Jesus.

Shutting the door to her room that night, Arabella sat in her chair, the favourite chair where she could look out the window. It was here that she was learning how to meet with Jesus. She had heard a visiting speaker say, 'Take your head off and put it under your arm. Look through the eyes of your heart.'

Arabella closed her eyes and mentally put her head under her arm. She felt a quietness settle over her; the busyness in her mind began to settle. "Jesus," she breathed out His name.

Eliora encouraged her. *'Say it again,'* she said. *'Keep saying His name.'*

"Jesus," Arabella breathed the beautiful name again. "Jesus," her mind settled, and silence descended. "Jesus," her heart responded as the physical realm began to part. "Jesus," her heart was now singing. And again, "Jesus."

She was there. With Him. Her heart reached out to the greatest love of all. Jesus. He put His hand out to her, and she took it. Together they walked through the mists that parted the physical to eternal realms. Her 'seeing' was still cloudy.

"It takes practice, my Arabella," He said. "We will meet every day, and every day as you practice my presence, you will start to see more clearly."

The vision faded, and Arabella was again in her bedroom. This time, though, her heart felt alive. The love of His presence continued to wash over her, just like the gentlest of waterfalls.

"Oh Jesus, I don't want you to go. I want to live with you forever." The longing to stay in that moment birthed in her the new phase, just as the Lord had said.

Arabella sat in her chair, looking over the garden, allowing the gentleness of Heaven to invade her entire being.

Eliora bowed to the Lord, for He was still there with Arabella, although she could no longer see Him with her spiritual eyes.

"The enemy is about to make another attack. Do nothing. I will not be far away. Nothing and nobody can snatch my warrior bride out of my hand," He instructed Eliora.

"Yes, Lord," she bowed before Him again.

Later that night, Arabella's sleep was restless. Eliora sensed the pure evil invasion, but the Lord had said He wouldn't be far away.

Tossing back and forth in her sleep, Arabella came face to face with the most beautiful Angel. The Angel beckoned to her, and she cautiously approached. The atmosphere plummeted to below Antarctic levels. Instantly, Arabella was transported into a dark place. The Angel did not touch her.

"Do you know who I am?" he asked her.

The answer rose unbidden without having to think about it. "You were once the most beautiful being ever created, the one who was known as Lucifer, the son of the morning. You who made war against Almighty God and lost. You are now known as sa-tan, the nameless one. That's who you are."

Lucifer made a show of clapping, applauding her knowledge. "But you know that I was given mankind. I was given the earth. Therefore, you are mine."

"Wrong on both counts. You coerced and fooled mankind into following you, and you have held the Earth captive ever since. But you forget, the one whose name is above all names, redeemed mankind and the Earth by His blood."

Was it her imagination, or did sa-tan shrink, lose some of his perceived stature?

"So you know your history. Well done." Curiously, he looked into her face. "Aren't you afraid of me?"

"Why would I be afraid of a being that has lost the war? Jesus disempowered you, your rulers and authorities, He made a public display of you, having triumphed over you through His death and resurrection."

He snarled at her response. "Oh, you think you are far smarter than me, but let me show you the regions of captivity I still hold."

Instantly, Arabella was in a hallway with doors leading off it, and above each door was written the name of the area of captivity. 'Fear' was above the first door.

Again he asked her, "Aren't you afraid of me?"

Again, unbidden into her mind came the answer. "Why should I be afraid of you? I am the righteousness of God in Christ Jesus."

Again, sa-tan seemed to shrink a little more. His beauty was fading. "Look at the next door Arabella. Then we will see how sure you are."

She read the sign over the door, 'The Mind.'

"Not so sure now, are you? Oh yes, I had you tormented in your mind until you lost your faith in *Him*," he spat the word out, barely even able to say it. "I am so powerful that I can even invade the minds of those who say they are Christians but whose minds are still corrupt," he sniggered.

Arabella looked at him in contempt before responding, "For who has known the mind of the Lord, that he may instruct him? But I have the mind of Christ." There was such assurance in her answer.

Sa-tan snarled, this time shrinking in front of her, his glorious garments starting to rot. "Sickness, then," he waved an arm in the direction of that door. "You can't say that He has conquered sickness because I ensure many get sick and die. This is MY domain," he shrieked at her.

She didn't even hesitate. "Yes, you have caused a lot of sickness, pain and suffering in the world and even among the true people of God, but by His stripes, I am healed." Again, Arabella quoted the scriptures.

Before sa-tan could confront her, Arabella moved to the next door that read 'Unbelief'.

Arabella stood looking at that door and, inwardly, had to acknowledge it was true. The Church was in great sin, in great unbelief. Silently, she asked the Lord for His answer to this, and again, just as He had promised, He gave her the answer. "For what if some did not believe? Shall their unbelief make the faith of God without effect?"

Sa-tan screamed in rage and dragged Arabella to the last door, which read 'Death.' You can't answer that, can you? There is no answer because anything you say would be a lie, and that would put you into my hand." He grinned in triumph, the facade of beauty now completely fallen away, revealing the rotting, disgusting stench of who he truly was.

Arabella didn't baulk. "For to me to live is Christ, and to die is gain," she responded. "Now, have you finished?"

Before the next door could be revealed, a low growl was heard. Sa-tan flinched.

The growl intensified as the padding of great paws was heard. The growl became a roar of an immense lion.

Sa-tan fled.

Arabella stroked the Lion's mane. "Thank you, Jesus. I knew you wouldn't leave me. Can I go home now?"

The Lion crouched down; Arabella climbed onto His back, feeling again the thrust of those tremendously powerful hind legs. "I could stay like this forever," she mumbled as sleep overtook her again.

The Lion watched over her for the rest of the night.

When she woke in the morning, His lingering presence had left the aroma of roses in her room. "Jesus," she murmured, "I love you."

Waking up in the morning was usually effortless, and Arabella would normally bounce into the new day with the zest of her young life. This morning was different. She grudgingly woke to the alarm calling her to rouse herself: Get ready for school; Wake! Awake! The world demands your attention. She hit the snooze button. And five minutes later, hit it again, until she could no longer ignore the passing of time.

"I'll be late for the bus," she moaned to herself as she reluctantly scrambled out of bed. She staggered into the bathroom and threw some cold water at her face, the shock of it helping her to become somewhat alert.

As the morning started, so the day followed. Arabella felt she was late for every class, and her body didn't want to move at its usual lively pace. She was unusually grumpy.

When she returned home from school, her customary call out to Evelyn was replaced by a muted grunt.

"What's wrong?" Evelyn asked her.

"Nothing."

"Okay," Evelyn responded. "So, if nothing is wrong, why aren't you talking to me?"

"I just don't want to talk, alright? Leave me alone!" Arabella shouted as she flounced out of the kitchen, trying to slam the soft-close door, and into the garden.

She stomped angrily through the garden, not aiming for any place in particular, just trying to escape the darkness that was following her. She plonked herself down behind the hydrangeas, which had come into leaf, bushing out to make an appropriate place in which to hide.

"Lord! What is happening? Why do I feel like this? I'm sorry, I've been grumpy all day. I was rude to Grandma. I feel bad. Jesus, I feel that there's something dark following me after that dream I had last night."

She sat hidden behind the hydrangea bushes, angrily brushing the tears off her face, trying to sort out the previous night's dream in her mind.

Eliora sat with her. From the times of the War in Heaven, she knew how the creeping evil could infiltrate and leave its cobweb of shadows clinging to one's back. She waited for Arabella to stop sulking and pray. Only then, could she start to brush off the darkness that had followed her from her night-time encounter.

Arabella heaved a great sigh. She hung her head and allowed her thoughts to go through the events, sorting and sifting, finally seeing the pieces fitting together. The deep evil; The confidence she had felt even when sa-tan was taunting her. Matthew 10 verses 19 - 20 popped into her mind. *But when they hand you over, do not worry about how to respond or what to say. In that hour, you will be given what to say. For it will not be you speaking, but the Spirit of your Father speaking through you.'*

Arabella felt the jolt of realisation course through her as she understood. "OH!" she exclaimed, and jumping up, ran inside.

"Grandma!" she called, "Grandma, I know what it is." She ran and put her arms around Evelyn. "Oh, I'm so sorry for being rude. Let me tell you all about it. But first, I want to pray.

"Jesus, I ask your forgiveness for my grumpy mood and being rude to Grandma." Arabella left a momentary pause before continuing, "In the name of Jesus… Yeshua, who is the Christ, the Anointed One of God Almighty, I put the Blood of Yeshua between myself and the darkness trying to smother me." She put her head to one side as though listening, and a slow smile spread across her face. "I say to the powers of darkness that I resist you. You must flee far from me, for I have the mind of Christ."

"Amen to that," Evelyn exclaimed.

Arabella laughed. "Thank you, Grandma, for loving me. I love you too."

CHAPTER TWENTY-SIX

The crescendo of praise reverberated throughout Heaven, with droplets escaping and falling onto those on earth whose hearts were Heaven-aligned.

Tina sat in her lounge room and heard the call to worship. She reached for her harp and started stroking the strings, and the notes escaped the strings and began their own worship to her beloved Papa.

Janet was painting the guest room as beads of liquid love fell drip, drip, drip, onto her hands. She smiled and started to hum while the pale grey paint caught the frequency and glimmered with the merest hint of dawn.

In her home, Lauren sat quietly, listening inwardly as the Blood of the Lamb flowed down and over her. She raised her one good arm towards Heaven in worship and started to sing. "Worthy are you, King of all Kings. Holy, Holy are you."

From under the Throne of God, the Blood flowed, and all in its path were changed. The Lamb stood tall as the frequency of His blood shattered the lies of the enemy, blasting apart the control of many minds, starting them on the journey to freedom.

Arabella was in her room, settling her heart, ready to practice getting into the presence of Jesus. She opened her Bible to Genesis four and started reading. It was a passage she knew well, but when she came to verse 10, 'The Lord said, "What have you done? Listen! Your brother's blood cries out to me from the ground," she stopped reading.

"Lord," she asked. "What does this mean? How can blood speak?" Her Bible lay open in her lap as her mind grappled with the seemingly impossible.

Eliora gave her the answer. *'Even the stones would cry out...'* She waited for a moment before saying, *'the mountains and hills will burst into song before you and, and all the trees of the fields will clap their hands.'*

Arabella closed her eyes. The Bible verses tumbled through her memory, stars singing, trees clapping, hills skipping like little lambs, and blood speaking? "But Lord, what does it mean?" she whispered, "I'm going to practice getting into your presence, Jesus. I want to know what this means, so I'm going to take my head off and put it under my arm and look through the eyes of my heart."

She sat quietly. As her restless mind quietened, her heart sought for the Lord. "Jesus," she said once. "Jesus," again.

"I'm never far, my Arabella. I promised you that I would never leave you." The perfume of His presence filled her breath until she saw a picture in her heart of an orange. Without being told, her heart knew that Jesus was there, right in her room. He smelt of fresh, delicious oranges.

She sniffed delightedly, trying to pull as much of that aroma into her lungs and heart as she could. Somehow the smell was alive.

"Yes, Beloved," Jesus said, "Even aromas carry their own frequency. You asked me about how blood could cry out, and into your mind poured so many Bible verses that told you that even what man thinks of as an inanimate object, is built a frequency, a vibration of life."

While her spirit accepted what the Lord was saying, her untrained mind found it difficult to reason through. *I'll ask Grandma,* she thought.

She took her Bible with her, and as she ran down the stairs, she called to her mother. "Mum, I'm going to Grandma's. I need to ask her something."

"Sure, Honey," Niccola smiled. She and Joshua were so grateful for Evelyn's love and patience.

Toby lolloped after Arabella as she ran across the lawn to Evelyn's cottage. "Grandma," she called, not waiting for an answer, opened the door and went in. "I need to ask you something."

"Do you, now. I'll make you a drink, and we'll talk after that." Evelyn went into the kitchen to make the drinks. Yes, it was her time out, but Grandmothers were never off duty, were they? She counted this position as such a privilege, recognising that it was the Lord who had brought her here.

Arabella sat cross-legged on the sofa, her long legs showing no sign of the child she used to be. Evelyn sighed. They grow too fast. *Bella is almost 16,* she thought.

After putting their drinks on the coffee table, Evelyn settled into her own chair. "Right, so what do you need to ask me?" she asked, eyeing the Bible Arabella had brought with her.

"I was reading through Genesis tonight, and I read something that made me think. I don't know what it means. I asked Jesus, and He seemed to show me a lot of different verses, but I can't really see how they work together." She opened to Genesis 4 verse 10, and read it out loud. "What does it mean? How can blood cry out? I mean, it's just blood isn't it?" she shrugged.

Evelyn nodded. "Oh, yes. That is a difficult passage to understand until you understand how important blood is. We know that if you cut yourself badly and all your blood poured out of your body, then you would die, right?"

Arabella nodded.

Evelyn continued, "And if we know that without blood you are dead, then it seems to me that the life is in the blood. Before Yeshua's death, the people's sins were covered over by the blood of an innocent animal. That animal had to die so that the people could live. When Yeshua ate the last supper with his disciples, He said to them to drink the wine because it was His blood that was spilt so that they could have life. In Hebrews 9 verse 14, it says, '*How much more, will the blood of Christ, who through the eternal Spirit offered himself unblemished to God, cleanse our consciences from acts that lead to death, so that we may serve the living God.*' Did you notice that it talks about the blood in the present tense, not past tense? It even infers that the Blood of Yeshua is in the future tense. You really should read the entire chapter, Bella, Love. It's quite a difficult-to-understand chapter."

Arabella sipped her drink thoughtfully. "I don't really understand what you are saying, Grandma."

"Well, this is how I see it. Whenever we read about the Blood of Yeshua, it was a once-off occasion, right?"

Arabella nodded.

Evelyn said, "Prior to Yeshua dying for everyone, the High Priest had to take the life of an innocent animal and offer the blood for himself and for the sins the people had committed. This was the only way that sin could be covered over, and only once a year was the High Priest allowed into the Holy of Holies, and never without the blood. Remember that the curtain that separated the people from the Holy of Holies was ripped in half when Yeshua died. Yeshua's blood gave us permanent access to God Himself. And this wasn't a temporary thing, it was forever. He was fully man, being born from a woman, Mary, and fully God as His conception was brought about by a sovereign act of God, with God as His father. Therefore, His blood is pure. It is literally the blood of God Himself, and speaks for our sins forever. With all the other verses in the Bible telling us that everything God created has life, to me it seems obvious that blood spilt through murder, and that includes abortion, continues to call out, just as Yeshua's blood does. His blood is still powerful and always will be. It is by His blood this world is redeemed, and by His blood that the enemy must flee. Also, in Hebrews 12 verse 24, it says that Yeshua's blood speaks a better word than the blood of Abel. So, it says to us that His blood still speaks. Does that answer your question?"

Arabella nodded. "I think so, but I'm really going to have to think about it. Night, Grandma." She stood up and kissed Evelyn on the cheek.

Thoughtfully, Arabella made her way home and upstairs to her bedroom. "Yeshua," she whispered as she got ready for bed. "What does this mean? I don't really understand."

As Arabella slept, Eliora heard the trumpet sounding, for the King was coming. She knelt before Him.

Yeshua sat on Arabella's bed and called to her. "Come, my fair one, come away with me. I have something I must show you."

A meeting had been called at The Hinge of the Universe.

Arabella stood with Yeshua and watched as the sounds of heaven and earth merged. "What is this place?" she asked.

Yeshua replied, "This is from where, one day, my Father will roll up the heavens and the earth and then create a new Heaven and a new Earth. This is the place of confluence, the place where the sounds of Heaven and Earth resonate together. This is where you will learn about my Blood, and how Heaven and Earth work together."

A choir of Angels took their place at the front. The most glorious music emanated from them; some singing, while the instrumental parts of what they were singing appeared to come from deep inside some of the others. Yeshua pointed to where a woman was sitting near the Angels.

She appeared to be on earth, and yet she was also in Heaven. She was holding an Irish Harp.

The choirmaster nodded to her. Tentatively she plucked the strings, and as she did so, the notes coming from the strings became alive.

The woman watched in wonder as the music frolicked in joy. The notes danced closer to the choir. The choir was poised waiting, and as the notes touched on the Angels' faces, each Angel inhaled a note, threw their heads back, and roared the notes out.

The notes flew from the place of the Hinge, to the Earth where they circled, singing praises to

God. Creation, previously held in bondage through sin, listened and joined in with the notes until the glory of God covered the entire Earth.

Yeshua looked at Arabella, who had a confused look on her face.

He laughed, "Don't you yet understand, Arabella? You cannot separate the Creation from the Creator. Everything has our fingerprints all over it, our breath of life. All Creation resonates with my frequency. This is why Scripture says that 'even the stones would cry out,' and the 'trees clap their hands', and the hills gambol as little lambs. They are all living frequencies. They respond to the resonance of my voice."

Arabella put her head to one side, considering. "In science, they teach that all natural objects have their own vibration or resonance. And also, that human organs give out a vibration, a frequency. Science is finding that if they can find the correct frequency, that they may be able to make a damaged organ to heal itself. Is that what you mean?"

Throwing His head back, Yeshua roared with laughter. "Oh, oh that is so funny. Yes, that is exactly right. If man would only drop their stance of pride, they would find all that written in my Word. You see, it's MY frequency and mankind has yet to understand that just yelling 'in the name of Jesus' isn't the key, the key is to live in me; in me you live and move and have your being. Therefore, you move at the same frequency as my light. Come," He said, taking her hand.

And now they were standing in a very dark place. It was so dark, she could barely see Him.

"I want to teach you about my blood. The power of the blood. Watch what happens."

He said very softly, "My Blood."

The darkness rippled.

"My Blood," He said again.

Arabella watched the shockwaves of His voice announcing the Blood, coursing across the darkness.

"Now, I want you to say it, Arabella."

She cleared her throat a little nervously, and said, "The Blood of Je… Yeshua."

The waves rippled through the darkness, on and on and on.

"Do the waves ever stop?" she asked.

"No. My Blood speaks for all eternity. Everything must make way for my Blood. It is just like the sounds the woman with the harp released continue to sound all the way around the earth, so my Blood speaks through all eternity."

Arabella nodded. That was easy to understand. "Why do you call yourself Yeshua? Isn't your name Jesus?" She asked.

"Oh, yes. My name is Yeshua. When it was translated from Aramaic to Greek to English, it was changed to Jesus. Most powers will bow to the name of Jesus, ALL powers will bow to the name of Yeshua. When the Blood is called into the realm of the Spirit, everything is forced to bow before it."

"You have learned much tonight, my precious child. I will be teaching you how to use what you have learned. But enough for now. You must sleep."

In her sleep, Arabella's mouth curved into a little smile.

Yeshua bent over and kissed her forehead. Eliora bowed before the King of Kings.

CHAPTER TWENTY-SEVEN

After months of deliberately seeking out Yeshua, and learning how to still her mind, Arabella had discovered a new depth developing in her relationship with Him.

She jealously guarded her precious time every night. Sometimes, she would read what she had written in her journal about her dreamtime adventures, and wonder about them. Now, she felt that she could not live without sensing His presence, and His presence was her barometer of her own state. If He felt distant, she knew that there was something in her blocking the freedom of companionship. Through this, Yeshua opened her understanding to those things that needed to change in her life. She learned new depths of humility.

As Niccola and Joshua watched their daughter grow in such grace, the awe they felt at being given such a precious gift brought them closer to God. Their angels rejoiced over a family at peace with one another and reflecting Heaven's original purposes.

Evelyn had always known, deep inside her, that her reason for even being on earth, was not finished. Even after David died, and through all the stages of grief, there had been something leading her on, urging her to look forward. She now knew what it was: to guide and teach this young girl in all she knew about God, Heaven, and the Spirit realm.

Arabella sat in her chair, with her Bible and notes she had scribbled down about love. "Today, Lord, I want to know more about your love. The obvious place is 1 Corinthians 13." She opened the Bible to the well-known passage about what love is and what it's not. "Hmmm, that's good, but it doesn't tell me about your heart, Jesus," she said out loud.

She continued through her love list, stopping at John 15 verse 13. *'Greater love has no one than this: to lay down one's life for one's friends.'* Allowing her thoughts to meander through the verse, considering all that had been done just for her, that someone, that is, Jesus, had literally laid his own life down for her. "I'm only fifteen, God, and I don't have any children, but I just can't imagine sending my only child, knowing they would die, for a bunch of people who don't even care. How could you do that? I can't even think about such love like that."

Arabella closed her eyes and tried to understand what huge love God had, that He and Yeshua would willingly do what they did. Her heart grew softer and opened wider to look at this remarkable truth.

Almighty God listened to the heart of His child. It was just for this purpose that He had done all He had. Reaching down, He pulled back the tiniest corner of eternity, showing the merest fraction of His powerful love to Arabella.

Instantly! Arabella's mind and body reacted in terror and fear, seeking a place to hide, while her spirit yearned for more. The juxtaposition of flesh versus spirit very obvious.

A groaning from deep inside Arabella urged its way from the depths of her being, out through the gate of her mouth. Tears streamed down her face. The overwhelming love of the Father, the Son, and Holy Spirit brought into sharp clarity. The small child concept of 'Jesus loves me' was blown apart, expanding until her mind saw the detail of the universe and every star, every grain of sand on the beaches, was imbued with intricate detail and love. Such love.

"Oh, Jesus… Yeshua. You already knew, didn't you?" she said, "You knew what was going to happen to you, and you still came to this earth, among so many people who didn't care at all. You became the bridge between God and mankind, just for me."

The Spirit of Understanding was touching Arabella, opening her eyes to see so much more than lay on the surface. Knowledge put her hand into Understanding's hand and together they touched this young woman.

Yeshua sat on Arabella's bed and smiled. Oh, His heart was overflowing with tenderness and love toward her. His promised Bride, watching as she grew. He called her softly, demanding her utter adoration for Him.

Arabella's heart heard. Her Spirit yearned towards the Bridegroom. She stood up with her arms upraised, everything in her craving to be one with Him.

Gently, His presence surrounded her, holding her.

She felt Him. Everything that she was, surrendered to His love. And they stood there, with His arms around her, as a protective shield, while she gave her life in its entirety to the King of all Kings. The High King. A child adopted by God, covenanted by blood, promised to each other for eternity.

"Yeshua," Arabella whispered, "I can't live without you."

"This is only our beginning," the Lord spoke to her heart.

Arabella sat down. Her legs felt unsteady, her heart so very full. "Will I ever be able to live in this love, Lord?"

She slept very well that night. Dreamless and deeply, waking refreshed and responding immediately, as her alarm insisted she awake.

CHAPTER TWENTY EIGHT

"Grandma," Arabella said, "when I share with the other kids at Youth Group all the things that Jesus-Yeshua shows me, it's as though they can't understand a word I'm saying. I told them about meeting Jesus by the stream, when I came out of the forest. They told me it was a nice dream." Arabella stared at nothing, seeing again the group of young people. "I don't understand, Grandma. You talk about your experiences with Yeshua, and I tell you and others about what He shows me, but they don't get it."

Evelyn nodded. She said, "1 Corinthians 3 verses 1 - 2 comes to mind:

'Brothers, I could not address you as spiritual, but as worldly—as infants in Christ. I gave you milk, not solid food, for you were not yet ready for solid food. In fact, you are still not ready, for you are still worldly. For since there is jealousy and dissension among you, are you not worldly? Are you not walking in the way of man?'

"Does that explain it?" Evelyn asked.

Arabella nodded. "But Grandma, a lot of them are older than me. They say they have always known Jesus, and they didn't go off in a different direction like I did. So why don't they understand?"

"Because their minds are not open to the truth. That's why," Evelyn stated emphatically. "They are like big babies sucking their thumbs. But you, Arabella, YOU have been given a great gift. Make sure you use it wisely."

Putting her afternoon tea dishes in the dishwasher, Arabella gave Evelyn a kiss on the cheek, picked her school bag up, and went upstairs to do her homework.

Evelyn wiped a tear off her cheek. "Lord, you are so good to me. Thank you for the joy of walking with Bella," she whispered in the empty kitchen.

Later that evening, when Arabella sat in her chair, taking that precious time out to seek after the face of Yeshua, she felt His gentle presence, reassuring, soothing and confirming, '*I am here, I will never leave you.*' "Thank you, Lord. Sometimes it's so hard, and I feel so alone. Thank you for Grandma, who understands."

As the peace of love settled on her, she could feel the tensions of disappointment and being misunderstood leaving her. The reassurance of love steadied her focus back onto the Lord and allowed her to just sit, feeling Heaven's presence washing over her and lifting her up again.

Joy bubbled and welled from deep within. As she drifted off to sleep, that giddy joy continued its healing.

The next morning, even the bus ride to school felt joyful, and she was almost skipping on her way to her homeroom.

The teacher called the class to attention. "We have a new student who has just moved into the area. Arabella, you have similar classes, so would you please buddy-up with Safiyya." The teacher indicated a girl with obvious Middle-Eastern ancestry. "Right, off to your classes. I'll see you tomorrow."

Safiyya shyly approached Arabella. Her eyes were an astonishing green, contrasting with her olive skin. Arabella had a startling feeling that she had met the other girl before. "What is your first class?" Arabella asked her.

Safiyya handed her the timetable and stood looking awkward.

Arabella read the first few lines. "Good, we're in the same classes until lunchtime. We'd better go, or we will be late."

Safiyya looked immensely relieved. "I was so afraid I would get lost. Thank you." She spoke with a strange accent.

Safiyya and Arabella sat together during the lunch break, quietly eating their lunches.

"Where did you live before?" Arabella asked.

"Syria," Safiyya said. "We are refugees. This is

my first time at school since we arrived. I am afraid my English will not be good enough. Thank you for being my friend."

"Wow," Arabella responded. "Your English is really good, how did you learn it? I've never known anyone who is a refugee. That must have been rather hard. Tell me more," she fired the questions at Safiyya.

Eliora smiled at Safiyya's Angel.

"Do you think my English is good? Mama and Baba insisted I learn. They speak English very well because they trained as medical doctors in Britain," Safiyya's face clouded with painful memories of home. "But I need to ask you if you know of a church that is truly for people who follow Jesus because we went to some when we were in the refugee centre, and I couldn't find Jesus in those churches." Safiyya slouched forward, defeat in her stance.

"Are you a Christian? Oh, I'm so excited!" Arabella exclaimed, "So am I. Yes, I can tell you. You could come to church with us. And youth group. Safiyya, I'm so happy that the teacher asked me to be your buddy. Wait till I tell Mum and Dad and Grandma."

The school bell signalling the end of the lunch break sounded.

"Come on," Arabella stood up. "We'd better go or be late for the next class."

After school that day, Arabella felt giggly happy, and when she got home, as she recounted the story, her words tripping over each other in their eagerness to be expressed. "Grandma, I'm so happy to have finally found a friend who genuinely loves Jesus." She stopped talking for long enough to eat her afternoon tea. "You know, it's strange, but when the teacher introduced us to each other, it was as though I already knew her."

Evelyn smiled at that one. "Oh, it's quite possible that you have met her before you came to be born. After all, none of us really knows what happens in Heaven beforehand, do we?"

Later, when Arabella was in her quiet place, she thanked the Lord for bringing Safiyya to her. "I've been so lonely, Lord," she told Him. "Thank you for Safiyya. Thank you, Father."

In the morning, as she scurried around getting ready for school, Arabella interrupted her mother's morning coffee. "Mum," she said.

Niccola looked over the rim of her cup. "Mmm?"

"Could we have Safiyya and her family over for a barbecue on Saturday? They are looking for a church, and maybe they could come to ours. We could be their first friends."

Niccola smiled warmly at her. She loved the warmth and generosity in her daughter. "I think that would be a great idea. Ask Safiyya today and find out how many are in her family. Suggest they come over at four, and we can get to know them before we eat."

"Thanks, Mum," Arabella yelled as she ran out the door to catch the school bus.

Arabella didn't have a chance to catch up with Safiyya until the lunch break. She looked at Safiyya's lunch with interest. "What is that?" she asked, pointing to some rolls.

"Shawarma wrap, my mother made them."

Arabella held her sandwich up, comparing the uninteresting look of bread to the exotic difference of another culture's cuisine. "I don't think I want my sandwich anymore," she said. "Safiyya, would you and your family like to come for a barbecue on Saturday night?"

"You would do that for us?" Safiyya asked. "My parents would like to meet you. I have talked to them about you."

"Oh, that's great." Arabella jumped up in excitement. "Mum said to ask how many of you there are."

Safiyya went very still, rigid. Her eyes reflected the dullest day. "There are only the three of us," she said in a choked voice. "I had an older brother, but because we are Christians, ISIS killed him. That's why we had to leave."

Eliora bowed her head. The blood of the martyrs was a strong fragrance to the Lord. Safiyya's Angel shone with a luminescence that the voices of the martyrs bring.

Arabella looked at Safiyya in horror. Nothing, absolutely nothing, in her short life had prepared her for what Safiyya and her family had been through. Wordlessly, she put her arms around Safiyya.

Heaven watched love enfold pain and dissipate it. The martyrs under the throne raised their hands in worship. Yeshua's fragrance enveloped both girls, sealing an eternal bond between the three of them.

From under the Throne of God, the Blood started to flow freely, and all in its path were changed. The ground on which Arabella and Safiyya stood was sanctified, purified by Jesus' precious Blood.

The school bell fragmented the suspended moment. Reluctantly the girls collected their things and went to their classes.

It was a silent bus ride home that afternoon. The enormity of what Safiyya had shared broke apart the shell of her safe world.

Quietly she opened the door to her house. The charcoal feeling around her pushed back the childlike curtains and exposed burgeoning adulthood. In the very dim alcove of her understanding lay grief.

If Evelyn noticed Arabella's silence, she said nothing. She knew that Arabella would talk when she was ready.

As Arabella finished her afternoon tea and collected her school things ready to take upstairs, she gave Evelyn a tight hug and kiss.

Something is definitely up, Evelyn thought.

Upstairs, Arabella put her books for homework on her desk. Her heart sat in a still quiet place, a sombre dawning of understanding. She opened her laptop and searched for Bible verses on martyrdom. She found Revelation chapter 6. "Is it true, Lord?" she muttered. "It's a dangerous business knowing you, Jesus."

Arabella recounted Safiyya's story over dinner. Her parents' horrified faces reflected her own response. *So that's why you were so quiet*, Evelyn thought.

The rest of the week folded its days noiselessly, seemingly aware of the damage *that* day had done. At 4 pm on Saturday, when Safiyya and her parents arrived, Arabella and her family went outside to greet them. Joshua was immediately taken with the dignified man, his grey beard lending an air of refinement.

"Hello," said Joshua, "I am Joshua. We are pleased you could come here today."

Arabella grabbed Safiyya's hand. "Come on," she said, "let's go to Grandma's place, so she knows you are here."

"Um, excuse me, young lady, just wait until we have all introduced ourselves," Niccola said. She put her hand out to Safiyya's father. "I am Niccola;

people call me Nic."

He smiled, his dark eyes crinkling at the corners. "I am pleased to meet you, Arabella's mother, Nic, I am Orhan, and this is my wife, Rana."

Though it seemed impertinent in the Arabic culture for a woman to take the lead, Orhan had learned enough to understand things were different in Western Society.

Rana put her hand out for Niccola to shake but was instead enveloped in a hug. Arm in arm, the two women went into the house.

Safiyya and her parents are just delightful, Niccola thought to herself. She and Joshua had decided that today would be a time of the stark reality of agape love, no matter how difficult. This family had desperate wounds, and if they could assist in the healing, they would do all they could.

Niccola led them all out to the back patio, where Evelyn had set the table with pre-dinner nibbles and drinks. So, the next couple of hours, the two families reached out tentatively, in a hesitant dance of getting to know each other.

Evelyn was quiet, but inwardly she was praying, for she sensed a fulcrum moment was hanging, waiting to be revealed.

If only those present could see it, this was a pivotal point for all. Among the many Angels were also some of the Cloud of Witnesses, including the martyred son of Orhan and Rana.

Yeshua nodded to the Angel of the family. "It's time," He said.

Joshua cleared his throat. "Bella told us that your son had died." He was being as tactful as he could, never his strong point.

The Angels waited for Orhan to speak.

Safiyya bowed her head. Her mother sat motionless.

Orhan's face reflected intense grief before he started speaking. "Our son had been at church. You must understand that in such strict Muslim culture, to be anything not Muslim is very, very dangerous. We had to meet in secret. It wasn't always this way. But when ISIS overran our country, freedom was stolen. Many Christians were killed, and my son Ghazi was one of them. They crucified him and many others."

Arabella put her hand on Safiyya's shoulder. She could feel her friend shaking. Rana gave a sob.

No one spoke. There was nothing to say.

The Angels gathered about the family and ministered to them.

Yeshua stood by Orhan. "Tell them about your experiences, my son," He said.

Orhan struggled to regain his equilibrium. "We knew then that we had to leave Syria. But to be seen to want to leave was death, especially for Christians. Many of us met secretly. We prayed. Oh, how we prayed. It was at this time we really started to search in the Bible, to really want to know Jesus. Before, for many of us, our religion had been what we did, not who we were. We were either Catholic or Orthodox; christened as babies, first holy communion, but very little knowledge or relationship with Jesus. We were Orthodox; our parents were Orthodox; their parents were orthodox, as far back as anyone knows. We thought that made us Christian. But ISIS and persecution... it changed us all. As we read through the Bible, we found things we had never been taught."

"Like what?" Joshua interrupted.

"Like how Jesus walked through walls; how He moved from one place to another without transport; like how Moses and Elijah appeared; like how some of the Apostles were able to move without transport, and even how Paul, though he was absent in the body, was present in the spirit. We learned about it all. And it happened to us."

"What do you mean, it happened to you?" Evelyn asked. There was urgency in her query. Arabella looked at her strangely.

Orhan smiled broadly. "Oh, yes. We found that what Jesus says, Jesus means. That John 14 verse 12 is true. *'Truly, truly, I tell you, whoever believes in Me will also do the works that I am doing. He will do even greater things than these, because I am going to the Father,'*" Orhan quoted. "Yes, one day, we were all gathered together to pray. It's not safe to do that, you understand. The person who was on watch suddenly screamed, and men with guns had us all surrounded. We knew then that we were going to be killed. So, we all started calling on Jesus. How it happened, I do not know, but all of us were picked up, and we found ourselves a few streets away from where we had been. Later, we found in Ezekiel 11 verse 24; it says that the Spirit of God picked Ezekiel up and carried him away to another town." Orhan shrugged. "It wasn't the only time. We knew that without the help of the Holy Spirit of God, that we would all be dead."

Arabella was riveted. Her spirit leapt at the supernatural encounters of her new friends.

"We have all read of these things happening but have never, until now, that is, known anyone who had actually experienced them," Evelyn said.

Rana leaned forward. "As the children of God start to realise who they are and mature to become sons, there will be more and more of these happenings. It's not just for a special few. But there are not many people we can share these things with." Rana's eyes were moist, naked longing in her face. "We have felt so... squeezed? in the things of God since we came to live in a safe country. You do not know how very blessed you are with your freedom. And the Christians in this country are asleep." She clenched and unclenched her hands. "We are very grateful to have met you. And Arabella, you are a gift from God for Safiyya."

Long hours later, after their guests had left, Arabella lay in bed thinking about all she had heard. She knew; she just KNEW that she had been handed a key. "Lord, but what does all this mean? How does it fit in?"

Eliora smiled as Arabella drifted into sleep. *Oh,*

if only she knew just how much more there was, she thought.

Over the next few months, after hearing about Safiyya's and her family's incredible experiences, Arabella felt quietly perturbed. She sat every night with the Lord, seeking His heart, and asking questions. "Why don't we hear about this sort of thing happening here, Lord?" There didn't seem to be any answer.

"Yeshua, I want to experience this. I love the times we spend together. I love the amazing things you have shown me. But I have never healed anyone. I have never raised anyone from the dead, and I have never walked through walls, or seen Angels, or anything of these things that seemed to be so commonplace. Why?"

There still didn't seem to be any answer from Heaven.

As present became future, Arabella's heart ached, wanting to know more, but there were seemingly no answers. Instead, she turned her focus to turning 16, and the remaining two years of her schooling ahead of her. So many decisions to make. What courses to take, which would lead to where she wanted to make her career. But which career? What did she want to do? At 16, getting older seemed to be an infinity away, yet school demanded her compliance.

"Have you had any thoughts about a career, Bella?" Joshua asked his daughter over dinner one day.

The thought of having to decide her entire future when she was only 16 years old was distressing Arabella, but an idea was glimmering in the back of her mind. "You know our friends in India with the children's home, Dad?" She spoke slowly, thinking and sifting through her thoughts as she spoke, seeing the seeds of light on each idea forming into a path forward.

"I think I would like to be a nurse and specialise in children's medicine. But maths and science are my worst subjects."

Joshua nodded, and from his peripheral vision, noticed Niccola smiling. "Well, I guess we shall have to work together on those subjects. After all, studying nursing isn't so different to studying to be a veterinary surgeon. Proud of you, girl. Well done."

Feeling as though an immense burden of pressure had lifted off her, Arabella slept very well that night. Her way ahead suddenly seemed easy.

CHAPTER TWENTY-NINE

Heaven's Council was called to session.

The Twenty-Four Elders were at the front, and the Angels bowed respectfully to them.

Heman signalled to the choir, which hummed with unrestrained melody. The music was sung into all the realms of Heaven. As the notes resounded into the surroundings, they fell as precious gems onto the ground, reflecting the rainbow colours around the throne of God. The gems cried out their praises to God.

The worship was living. It had its own resonance, which alighted on whoever and whatever was in its path. Everything sang in worship to the King.

Times beyond time and all in between, the worship and praise rang through the realms sweeping all before it. The second heaven cringed as they heard the hated sound, once so familiar and beautiful.

Those in Council breathed in the fragrance of apples and cassia as it filled the room. The Twenty-Four Elders threw their crowns on the ground in worship. The King had arrived.

He walked to the front of the room, indicating His pleasure at their love. "My beloved family," He started, "we have met many times before, but now this meeting is critical for all of mankind. Now is the time for the Sons of God to be revealed. It is your responsibility to ensure they understand who they are. I have visited them all and will continue to do so. As the scales of deception fall off them, then I will be able to talk face to face with them." Yeshua wiped a tear off His cheek. "I have longed for this time, and you well know how few are even seeking me, let alone yearning for close fellowship with me." He smiled at them, the radiance of that smile alone lighting up vestiges of darkness in the outer courts, and then held His hands up so all could see the names of His loved ones engraved on the palms of His hands.

The Angels and the Twenty-Four Elders bowed before Him as He left the room.

Busyness of chatter and debating filled the chamber. Angels and the Elders spoke over the top of each other, each full of ideas and enthusiasm, and Scribes calling out for the babble to slow while they caught up.

For such a time as this. They had been called into formation long ago; each knew their place and knew what was expected—the implementing of the glorious long-awaited plan.

There was a restlessness on earth. Arabella sensed it. She and Safiyya had started praying together and encouraging each other. When they read in 1 Timothy 4:12 how Paul told Timothy not to let anyone look down on him just because he was young, they felt their faith grow again.

Eliora saw the growth as well. And if Eliora had seen it, so had hell. And hell took notice.

Nightly, Arabella sat in her chair and queried the Lord. "Where are you. Why can't I see you? Where are the miracles, and signs, and wonders? You said that we would do greater things than you, Jesus, but we can't do anything! Why?"

In the new year, sometime after her birthday, Arabella was pacing in her room, the desperation to know Yeshua closely, causing her to cry out. "Yeshua, where are you? Everything in me is longing for you, to see you, to know you." The longing to know Him in a deeply personal way formed a deep well of hunger, with a craving that fought to be satiated.

Eliora gently touched her shoulder and said, "Arabella, sit down. Open your heart to praise the King."

Though she neither heard nor saw Eliora, Arabella sensed the need to be still. She sat in her 'prayer chair', as she called it now, and closed her eyes. A song came to mind, its melody floating along, and Arabella started to sing the words quietly. "Holy, holy are you, Lord God Almighty."

"Sing it again, Arabella," Eliora said.

As words and melodies glided together, the intensity of Arabella's yearning turned inward to a heart's cry of love. She was no longer conscious of earth, all in her now being opened to the realms of Heaven. The long months of deliberately seeking Yeshua took over, and her heart and spirit wound together and ascended towards Yeshua.

On the inner screen of her mind, she found a garden gate. There was no hesitation, just confidence that she would be welcome. Oh, the aroma, the scent of fresh oranges. She sniffed. Another delicious smell. Oh! Honeysuckle. Opening the gate, she walked through the walled garden toward where she could hear the sound of trickling water. As she walked, she noticed that the path glowed as if it were lit from underneath.

All around her were birds and flying insects. They were friendly, eager to see this visitor to their garden. Deeper into the garden, along the golden path, the sound of water becoming clearer.

As she followed the path around a corner hidden by tall shrubbery, she came to a space, a clearing. There was the water trickling in the pond, a seat, and a man with His back to her.

Her heart reached out to this man. He seemed familiar, her lover. He whom she had longed for. And she ran to Him. "Yeshua, I finally found you!"

He turned around and held His hand out to her, leading her to sit on the garden seat. "Arabella," He said, "I have longed for this time, until you were mature enough. Beloved, we have much to talk about."

"Lord," she cried, her face wet with tears, "I have called for you, wanted to see you for so long. You didn't answer me. Why didn't you answer me?"

He smiled; that smile that lights the entire universe. "I have been answering, Arabella. You have not seen my answer because the eyes of your understanding have been closed. We have much to talk about, and you have much to see. Take my hand," He said.

She took His hand and found herself in a different place.

"This is my viewing room," He said. "Here I am going to show you the answers to all the questions you have been asking me." He waved His hand at a wall, which instantly parted, showing a dark space that seemed to have extraordinary depths.

Looking deeply into the dark space, she started to notice differing shades of darkness, and as each of the shades blended into another, there were what looked like ribs, but the ribs ran around the entire internal circumference of the blackness. "It's like a wormhole in a space movie," she said.

"That's an excellent description for what you are looking at. It is, in fact, time and distance. I am going to show you the reason why my Church is so powerless today. Why most of my people do not see what you have been privileged to see."

"Time, part!" He commanded the darkness.

They sat and watched together as time gave way.

Arabella leaned forward, her chin resting on her hand, brow furrowed in concentration as she watched. People, ordinary people, going about their lives. That they were filled with the Holy Spirit was evident, for when they spoke healing over people, the healing happened. Many were delivered from demons. She watched as limbs were straightened, and missing limbs grew again. Sickness and disease collapsed as the name of Yeshua was spoken. She clapped spontaneously in delight, as not just one or two, but a lot of people were picked up by the Spirit of God and transported to another place. Sometimes, it was to save them from danger, and other times to bring the amazing good news about Yeshua to others.

But there was another side to the glorious happenings. Even as the Church grew and believers started to cover the known world, persecution was rife.

Cringing as whole families and communities were decimated, sold into slavery, and many killed, Arabella wept. But as each life was snuffed out, something remarkable happened. Rather than the Church running to hide, they became bolder, their lights getting brighter, and like dandelion seeds floating and growing elsewhere, their deaths caused the gospel of Jesus Christ (Yeshua the Messiah) to explode throughout the entire known world.

For three hundred years, the terminology of wildfire was most apt. Persecution could not kill the new Church. It only strengthened it.

A new ruler rose on the earth with one desire: to conquer and control everything. The Roman emperor ruthlessly decimated people in his quest for power. Christianity had to either bow to him or die. Martyr after martyr took their place under the throne of God. The prayers of the saints filled the golden incense bowls, which were poured out before the throne.

Hell cackled in unholy glee at the devastation and lives destroyed until it realised that rather than destroying the seed of the Son, they were causing an exponential growth. An urgent change of plan would need to be rapidly put into motion.

Arabella was fascinated by what she was seeing, recoiling from the discussions in hell, her heart's ache easing by what she saw next.

In AD312, Constantine started to favour the church. But he was a statesman. A strategist. He came up with a cunning plan. Rather than alienate all the religions of Rome, he started to cleverly integrate them into the new religion of The Way, this Christianity.

Looking at Yeshua, Arabella was surprised to see tears streaming down His face and saturating His beard.

"Lord!" she was shocked. "But the people aren't being persecuted anymore."

"Watch," was all He said.

She turned back to the viewing screen. Constantine considered how best to appease all the people and maintain his control over his empire. He called the weak church leaders together with the priests of the goddess Diana. Then he summoned the priests of Mithras.

"I have had a revelation from the God," he said, "I see now that the goddess Diana is Mary, the mother of Jesus."

There was a startled reaction from all the assembled religious leaders. But Constantine was adept at handling these situations. He held his hand up for silence. "Furthermore, I see that Mithras is no less than the representation of the birth time of the Christ. We will celebrate the birth of Christ on the feast of Mithras."

Constantine felt very pleased with his easy answer and the way in which he, the mighty Emperor, had stitched it all together. His answer had been to create a one-world religion, and it seemed to have brought peace. Then he set about to have men organise this religion called Christianity. In AD325, he invited every bishop, including Arius, to gather in Nicaea and establish Christian doctrine. There was much debate as to whether Jesus was indeed God. At first, they said He was, and then He wasn't.

A sob from Yeshua broke Arabella's concentration. She was aghast to see her beloved crying.

"But Yeshua, this brought peace. It stopped the people from being killed."

She could not understand His grief.

"Just watch," He repeated.

"Okay." Arabella turned her attention back to the screen. Peace settled on the peoples of the world. Where she had expected the people of God to blossom, the opposite happened. Arabella saw man organise themselves into religious groups, calling themselves Popes and Bishops, and setting up a system whereby through the ages, the people no longer knew what was written in the letters the Apostles and others had written, nor what the books of Moses nor the prophets said. They were taught to rely instead on what they were told. As decades turned into centuries, gradually, the glory of the Gospel of Hope was diminished with only a few people carrying the light.

The people were not told the truth of hope. They were taught to buy their salvation with money and penance. Truth was deliberately kept from them, for keeping people from knowing the truth meant they were easily controlled. Passover was changed into Easter to honour the goddess Eostre; the goddess of dawn and new life, celebrated by the giving and receiving of eggs.

Little by little, the light diminished in the church, with just a few flickering lamps seen. What had been a life of vibrancy, became a set of regulations; the people watched over and ruled by those who put themselves at the head of the Church. The hierarchy of the established church was now operating from a spirit of witchcraft;

dominating, manipulating and intimidating. The people dwelt under the density of religion.

The view through the viewing screen became shorter as time came closer. Fewer times of miraculous outpourings occurred, and if they did, they were fleeting. Arabella watched as Holy Spirit poured out beautiful anointing on trustworthy people, only to have it stolen within a generation and taken for another's gain.

Suddenly, the screen changed, and they were looking straight into hell, where there was great consternation. "Time is short, time is short," satan was screaming at the grotesque demons. "The Sons are rising. Stop them. Stop them now!"

Suddenly, a voice cried out TRUTH.

The surface of the earth heard the resonance and vibrated to the sound. The dullness over people's minds and spirits cracked open, and Truth danced with them.

Yeshua chuckled. Then He laughed, and then with great belly laughs, He roared with huge gulping guffaws.

Arabella was mystified, but it was funny watching Yeshua laugh so hard. It was contagious, and she, too, started laughing without knowing what the laughter was about.

And then, she saw. As Yeshua laughed, hell trembled. They were retreating, and suddenly, lights started appearing all over the earth, dot, dot, dot. Dotdotdotdotdot. Faster. Swiftly. It looked as though the lights were holding hands, joining together, rapidly covering the face of the earth. "Truth," they were all shouting, "We see the truth now. We have believed a lie and been taught unbelief. But the word of God is TRUE!"

At that shout, the facade of religion crumbled. The earth shook. The Sons of God took their place. They moved easily between the earth and Heaven, receiving their instructions and taking them back to earth, where they implemented what was written on their blueprints.

"The Sword of the Spirit of our God," they cried, all raising their swords in one hand. "The Word of God" became a mighty shout, and from their hands, issued lightning and power through the words they carried.

"Finish," Yeshua said, and the screen shut down, leaving Arabella staring at the blank wall.

She blinked several times, then looked at Yeshua, her face posed as a large question mark.

"What I just showed you, Arabella, was the plan of the enemy to destroy my Church. When they couldn't shut it down through persecution, they tried to destroy it through apathy and the control of man, misinformation and deliberate lies. But by my Spirit, I have overcome and what you saw at the end is what is to come. Even now, my Sons are rising. They are the hidden ones. The ones who choose to embrace all I have for them." He stopped speaking, looking at Arabella intently.

"Will you also be a Son, Arabella?" He asked.

The vision faded. Arabella opened her eyes to find herself still in her bedroom, still sitting in her chair. There was a strange tension in the room, as though there was an unanswered question.

Eliora stayed very still. She knew the question. She could not influence Arabella one way or the other. The decision had to come from inside Arabella alone.

"Will I be a son?" Arabella stood up and walked over to the window, staring at the trees starting to lose their leaves for winter. "A Son," she repeated. Turning abruptly, she walked to her desk and woke her laptop up. She typed into the search engine 'sons of God.'

Weird sites came up, but she scrolled down until she found what she was looking for. Romans 8:19, *'The creation waits in eager expectation for the revelation of the sons of God.'*

"Lord," she whispered. "Teach me. Yes, I will be a son."

CHAPTER THIRTY

No matter how hard she had to study, Arabella tried to never waver, though, from her time with Yeshua every day. That was sacrosanct, and the days she did miss it, she felt somehow less, as though a water supply was being restricted.

Juggling her school work and extra science and maths, alongside the revelation Yeshua had given her, stretched Arabella. But through it all, she found a determination growing. After making her decision to become a nurse, maths seemed, in some strange way, to become more logical. She deliberately concentrated on the maths and sciences, as she saw them fundamentally underwriting her future choices.

Through the months of summer, Christmas and her birthday, she and Safiyya grew closer. Safiyya fed Arabella's thirst for understanding the previously unknown ways of the Spirit of God. Together they would pray, seek out what had been hidden for so many centuries. Yet, there still seemed to be a point beyond which her faith did not go.

As May gave way to June, and late Autumn relinquished its control to winter, Arabella kept pushing harder to know more. The longer nights meant less time outside, more time available to deliberate.

That night after her homework was done, Arabella sat in her prayer chair and picked up her Bible. "Lord, for so long, I have been asking you the same question. You showed me a lot of the answers, yet still, I can't seem to break through to that place of complete intimacy with you."

Eliora nodded as the Twenty-Four Elders gave her direction. '*Study the four gospels, Arabella,*' she said.

Arabella picked her Bible up and flicked it open to the start of the New Testament. "Lord, if I read the four gospels, would you please open my understanding, show me what I'm missing?"

"Matthew, Mark, Luke and John. I have read all those before. Over and over, but I can't see it. Holy Spirit, I need you to show me." Arabella felt unusually despondent. "There doesn't seem to be any way forward!"

All she had been practising for the last year came back to her. Sit still. Stay your mind on Yeshua. Practice His presence.

She closed her eyes, startled to see a vision of the pages of her Bible flicking at speed and then stopping momentarily, just long enough for her to read the references that were highlighted.

Matthew 13:58
Mark 6:6
Hebrews 3:19

Arabella opened her eyes, scribbled down what she could remember of the references, then opened her Bible to the first one, Matthew 13:58. She read it quietly. "*And he did not many mighty works there because of their unbelief.*" Then turned to the next reference.

"Mark 6 verse 6," she muttered, flicking through the pages. '*And he marvelled because of their unbelief. And he went round about the villages, teaching.*'

Her heart started to beat faster, and she hurried to find Hebrews 3 verse 19. Arabella read it out loud, "*So we see that they could not enter in because of unbelief.*"

"What is the common theme, Arabella?" Yeshua asked her.

"Unbelief," she replied. "But I do believe, Lord."

"Do you?" He responded. "What about that time when you asked me to heal Violet, but deep inside, you only hoped I would heal her. And then the next time you asked me to do something, the unbelief had grown, and when you asked me to do that as well, you didn't really believe I would. Where does that unbelief come from?"

Deep inside Arabella, the substance of unbelief responded to the Master's voice but remained stubbornly hiding. Yeshua glared at it.

He asked Arabella again, "Where does that unbelief come from, Arabella?"

She shrugged, "I don't know. Because I honestly do try."

"Let's look, shall we?"

On Arabella's mind ran pictures of what she had been shown before. How the church was subjugated, brought into bondage and finally being shown with its light almost gone. Alongside those visions, Yeshua then showed her another recurring theme. Priests, Pastors, Ministers all teaching people to pray, "If it be your will, Lord, to heal this person." When the person being prayed for died, the people were taught, "It wasn't the Lord's will to heal them. They have entered into their rest."

Arabella nodded. "Yes, isn't that true, though?"

Yeshua looked at her very closely. "Show me in my Word, where I didn't heal someone, Arabella. If I recall correctly, I healed all who came to me. Not some, but all. So why now do you not believe?"

She just looked at him numbly. "I don't know. I just don't know."

"Did you know that to pray to me, 'Your will be done, Lord,' and not to believe that I will heal someone, is to call me a liar?"

Arabella was horrified. "But you aren't a liar! You are God; you cannot lie."

"Correct, so why do you not believe?"

She just sat there. "I absolutely do not know."

Before her eyes, Yeshua paraded a multitude of

generations, all sliding into unbelief until the kernel of unbelief was deeply embedded in all of mankind's DNA.

"This," He said, "Is why my Church today are powerless. They have believed many lies, and I am revealing those lies and who I am and who you are. For you are made in my image."

The vision faded, leaving Arabella stunned.

Her thoughts galloped, tearing down through the history lesson she had been given and splashing through streams of tears.

There was nothing left to do except fall on her knees in repentance, for yes, she was guilty of unbelief.

Eliora waited for Wisdom to give her the right words. And they came. "Arise, shine; for your light has come, And the glory of the LORD has risen upon you, Arabella."

Unbelief started to wither. It would take time for it to die, but Eliora knew that die it must, if the church were to rise.

CHAPTER THIRTY-ONE

Now that Arabella stood at the threshold, the battle of unbelief increased dramatically. Her childlike faith was tried at every point, forcing open the discussion within herself on what to keep and what was trash.

Eliora knew that if Arabella could stand and watch the battle going on inside herself, that she would be encouraged, for as she exercised her faith, the trash pile was growing.

"Grandma," Arabella said as she settled down for a long chat with Evelyn after school one day. "Why can't I just believe? I find myself knowing that all things are possible when I am looking at Yeshua, but when I look around me and find that nothing seems to have changed, then that unbelief seems to smack me in the face."

"Oh, how I understand that conundrum," Evelyn responded, "It seems to me that if I stand in the presence of the Lord, all things are possible, but when I am just looking at things through my own eyes, then I fall."

Arabella thought about that for a moment. "Mmmm, maybe. So why can't I just live like that all the time?"

"I don't know. Maybe it's the unbelief factor again. Because from what I read in the Bible, before sin, Adam and Eve lived like that," Evelyn paused, thinking for a while. "Unbelief has to be starved out. We can't deliver ourselves from unbelief. We need to feed faith and starve unbelief. Does that make sense?"

"Yes, yes it does," Arabella answered while gathering her school things together. "I'd better go and do my homework. Thanks for the afternoon tea, Grandma."

As much as she tried to keep her mind on her study, Arabella's concentration kept wandering off into the realms of belief and faith versus unbelief. With a sigh, she pushed her books to one side.

"How?" she asked the room, "Just how do you have more faith?" Staring out the window, she twirled her hair with a finger, tapping her pen on her teeth. "Ooh, hang on a minute." Flipping her laptop open, Arabella started searching. "Aha! Matthew 14, Jesus - Yeshua walked on the water and then Peter asked if he could." Her lips moved as she read the story; the hair twiddling slowed and finally stopped.

Eliora smiled.

"OH, WOW!" Arabella exclaimed loudly. "That's it! So, Lord, Peter was fine breaking all natural laws and walking on water while he was completely focused on you, but the second he suddenly looked at his circumstances, he figured he'd better start swimming instead. So, Peter looked at something that is inferior! Jesus, I really need to learn this."

Yawning, she put her schoolbooks away. "I need to go for a walk," she announced to the room and changed into some exercise gear.

Running down the stairs, she called to the dog, "Come on, Toby, let's go for a walk."

Evelyn looked up from preparing the dinner as Arabella grabbed an apple on her way out. "Be back before dinner is ready," she said, then inwardly chided herself, for she knew that as Arabella approached 17, she was well able to regulate her schedule. "It's hard to let them go, Lord," she sighed and turned her mind back to the vegetables.

Arabella and Toby walked to the local park, and then, breaking into a jog, she and the little dog did a circuit before slowing to a walk. Finding a park bench, she sat quietly, people-watching and enjoying the space to just sit. In the quiet time just sitting there, she felt at peace, where there were no demands, no homework; a place where all dimensions of time, space, Heaven and earth were still. That time between times when she recalled her visit to Yeshua's Garden. And it left her refreshed in her mind, her soul, her body.

"Toby, we had better go home, boy." She walked home, with the three-legged dog jogging along beside her. She let herself in through the kitchen door. "I'll go and shower, Grandma, and then feed the marauding tiger and the vicious canine."

Evelyn smiled at her description of the two family pets. While Saffie could use her claws, she was about as domesticated as a cat could be, and Toby, well, there was nothing vicious about the sweet little dog at all.

Arabella, refreshed and clean, walked into the kitchen, calling the animals. Toby bounced around her excitedly. There was no response from Saffron.

"Saffie," she called again while feeding Toby. When there was no answering plaintive Siamese cat yowl, Arabella went outside and called her again. "Saffie!" Arabella listened. Nothing. Walking to the garage, she continued calling her. "Bet you are locked in the garage." She opened the garage door and called again, "Saffie, you are missing out on your dinner."

Silence.

Arabella went back into the kitchen. "Grandma, I can't find Saffie. She usually demands her dinner. I've called her and looked in the garage. She's never done this before."

"I'm sure she will turn up. But I agree, it's not like madam Saffron to miss an opportunity to eat." Evelyn tried to be upbeat.

When her parents got home about an hour and a half later, there was still no sign of the cat.

Joshua went out to the street, looking in the gutters. He checked the garden shed, which was empty of any living thing except spiders.

"Let's have dinner," Niccola said, trying to bring the family into a sense of normality. "And we'll pray, alright?"

The four sat down for dinner, automatically holding hands while Joshua thanked God for the food and blessed it, then asked the Lord to protect their precious pet and return her safely.

Eliora, Janel, Abaigael and Asriel could only watch. They knew where the cat was. They knew this was the Lord's doing. "A plan and a purpose," Asriel said. The others nodded. It grieved them that their lovely people could not see and understand.

"It won't be long," Eliora said, "This has to happen to bring about the greater plans and purposes for Arabella's life."

"The Lord's ways are far above our ways," Janel said.

The four angels nodded. They understood.

"She has the cat door, we'll leave her food out, and I bet she'll be home when we get up in the morning." Joshua assumed the sensible veterinarian's role.

After dinner, with the dishes done and the kitchen swept, Arabella went to her bedroom. She knew she should do her homework, but her mind was on her missing cat. She pushed her books aside for the second time that day. "Lord, I can't concentrate. I'm so worried about Saffie. Please, show me where she is. Bring her home, Lord." She picked her water bottle up and drank, momentarily disengaging her mind from her anxiety. But it was enough time to allow her to refocus her thoughts. "Homework, I have to do my homework." The anxiety over the cat relegated behind schoolwork.

Two hours later, her work and study done, Arabella changed into her nightclothes, and sat in her prayer chair. Abruptly she stood up again and ran downstairs to the lounge room where her parents were watching TV. "Has Saffie come home yet?" she asked.

Joshua put his hand out and took hers, enfolding her little hand in his large, comforting fatherly grasp. "No, Honey. She hasn't yet. If she isn't home by tomorrow night, then we'll put some posters and fliers around the neighbourhood. And of course, I'll action it through the Animal Clinic." His eyes openly displayed his love for this child of his. "We have prayed; now we have to believe. Give me a hug, baby." He pulled Arabella onto his lap, and even though she was closer to adult than to child, she curled up in the security of his arms.

Three Angels smiled. What a wonderful reflection of the Father's heart for His children.

"Thanks, Daddy. I'd better go have my prayer time and then go to bed. Love you." She kissed her father and then her mother. Her heart was more at peace as she ran up the stairs singing.

Her parents smiled. "That's a good sign; I'll go and make us a drink," Niccola said, getting up and kissing her husband on the top of his head.

Abaigael and Asriel smiled. This was a good marriage. These two were doing their best to reflect Heaven on earth.

Arabella sat in her prayer chair with her Bible open at Matthew 14, reading again the account of Peter and Jesus walking on the water. "Father," she prayed, "Show me how this relates to praying for Saffie to come home."

Closing her eyes, she allowed the agitation to subside, and then feeling the peace of Jesus assuring her of His presence, she breathed out slowly, bringing her mind into subjection to the Spirit of God. Going through her routine of seeing through the eyes of her heart, Arabella felt the swell of glory rising in her, bringing to remembrance all that Jesus had shown her. Whispering praises to her Lord, she raised her arms to Him, adoration and surrender. "Yeshua," she whispered. The Angels in the room knelt as the weight of glory fell a little more.

"Lord, I love you." Delight played on Arabella's words. The motes of dust danced with the light from the lamp, while Arabella continued in her unspoken devotion and reverence to the Lord.

"Yeshua, thank you for caring for me, for every tiny thing that I care about. Nothing is too small and outside your hands. I am worried about Saffie. She is always here at this time. She wouldn't go without her food," Arabella laughed, "Where is she, Lord? Please bring her home. Lord, you have been talking to me about belief and faith. So, I am going to believe that you will bring her home. I am going to keep looking at you. This is going to be my statement of faith, that you know where Saffie is and that you will bring her home because you love me, and I have asked you to do this for me." Arabella remained in her position of loving Jesus.

Doubts and thoughts of the lost cat crept to the fringes of her mind, and she insistently pushed them away.

"You said that anything we ask in prayer, through Yeshua, the Father will answer, so that's my prayer tonight." Taking a deep breath, Arabella closed her Bible. "Time for sleep now, Lord."

In some ways, Eliora's heart was a little saddened, as she knew the battle that was ahead. But she also knew of the power this time of testing would bring.

"Sleep well, little one. The Lord God knows. He has a plan and a purpose. You can trust Him." Eliora glowed with the light of the Lord.

As soon as her alarm went off the next morning, Arabella scrambled out of bed and ran downstairs to look for the cat she was sure would have returned. She had asked Jesus; therefore, she was expecting her miracle.

Toby's nails clicked on the kitchen tiles as he followed her into the kitchen. Otherwise, all was very quiet. Saffron's food was untouched.

Unbidden tears stung from the corner of Arabella's eyes. No Saffron.

"Lord," was her only word as she dejectedly made her way back upstairs to get ready for school.

All during that long day, she refused to allow the darts and words coming into her mind. The hissing of 'She's never coming back. She's dead. You are foolish for believing.' Stubbornly, Arabella dismissed the thoughts. She and Safiyya prayed together at lunchtime.

"Again, I say to you that if two of you agree on earth about anything that they may ask, it shall be done for them by my Father in heaven. For where two or three have gathered together in my name, there I am in their midst." Safiyya declared, quoting Matthew 18:19.

"Amen," Arabella agreed with her.

Forgetting she was no longer a child, as soon as Arabella got off the school bus that afternoon, she ran into the house, calling for the cat. "Grandma," she asked Evelyn, "Has Saffie come back?"

"No, Sweetheart, I'm sorry. I haven't seen her."

"That's ok, Grandma. I have prayed, I have asked Jesus to bring her back, so she will come back." Her stubborn faith persisted, though the storm threatened.

All afternoon and into the evening, Arabella forced her entire focus to be on Yeshua. "I am trusting you, Lord," she said over and over.

The following day, she got out of bed a little more slowly but full of determination and made her way downstairs to look for the cat. Once again, she wasn't there.

Joshua came into the kitchen. "We'll do some flyers and posters, and you can put them in letterboxes after school today. If she's," hastily Joshua changed what he had been about to say. "If she's been seen," he amended, "People will tell us."

Nodding, Arabella slowly went upstairs. Unbelief started prodding her. She obstinately pushed it away, whispering, "Lord, I believe. I believe. Help me to believe, Yeshua." Deep inside, she knew she had nothing left, nothing of her own. "Yeshua, I can't hang on. I'm empty, Lord."

Time seemed paused, minutes stationery. Her anxiety to get home and check on her cat again caused a lack of concentration in class. "I'm sorry," she apologised when a teacher remarked on her lack of mindfulness over Biology.

When the school day finally came to an end, Arabella felt nervous going into the house. Maybe God wasn't listening. Maybe Saffron wasn't going to come home. Maybe she was dead. That thought caused an involuntary sob. Nonetheless, she put a mask of belief on and went inside.

Before she could ask, Evelyn just shook her head. "I'm sorry, Love. But here, your father printed these fliers out. Have your afternoon tea and then go and put them in every letterbox.

Picking one of the fliers up, Arabella saw the

beautiful photo of Saffron taken out the back, under the plum tree. The blossoms had fallen off the tree and created a carpet around her. Arabella ran her thumb over the photo. "Come home Saffie, I miss you so much," she murmured. "I'll go and get changed, Grandma, and then have my afternoon tea, so I can go straight out and put these in the letterboxes. I'll take Toby with me so he can have a walk."

One hundred letterboxes had the photo and details of Saffron poked into their yawning mouths. People on the street had the photos shown to them. Head after head shook sadly with 'sorry, no, I haven't seen her. I hope you find her.'

Dejectedly, Arabella walked home again.

Unbelief whispered, "See, it didn't work. You said you would believe, but it hasn't worked."

"I will believe," Arabella said out loud, startling old Mrs Caetano in her garden. "But Father, I can't believe by myself."

That night, Arabella moved restlessly around her bedroom, praying every type of prayer she had ever heard. "Lord you said, 'And whatsoever you shall ask in my name, that will I do, that the Father may be glorified in the Son. If you shall ask anything in my name, I will do it.' So, I'm asking now in your name, Yeshua, that you bring Saffie home again." She stood still for a moment, thinking. "Oh, and I thank you. Please. Thank you. Amen."

The accuser swiftly threw another dart at her mind. "You are trying to manipulate God."

Eliora's lips thinned as she recognised the accuser, but she knew the blueprint that was being played out. Then as she heard Heaven's beauty talking, she threw a thought to Arabella. "In everything, give thanks, for this is the will of God in Yeshua the Messiah concerning you."

The thought pierced the barb of the enemy, and Arabella caught it. "Yes, I will thank you, Lord, even though I don't see your answer, I will thank you. So, thank you that you are bringing Saffie back."

It was about 2 am when Arabella woke up. Hesitantly, she felt on her bed with her feet, feeling to see if a warm lump had arrived and gone to sleep on the end of the bed. All her feet encountered were the cool sheets.

Instantly the attack came again. "It didn't work, did it? You don't have enough faith."

The tears, before held back, now breached her stubborn resistance.

In her bedroom, Niccola awoke at the sound of her daughter's crying.

"What's wrong?" Joshua sleepily asked.

"Sssh, I'll go to her. She is really grieving about Saffie." Niccola got up and put her robe on, quietly walking across the hallway to Arabella's bedroom. She sat on the bed and just held her daughter. So nearly grown, yet still needing her mother. "Baby, we can only trust Jesus, hang onto His faith. He knows where Saffie is. And Bella, if Saffie isn't coming home, then we know that she is with Him.

Safe, with Him."

Arabella's sobbing slowed. She had to acknowledge what her mother had said. "Thanks, Mum. I'll be okay, now."

She lay awake thinking, after her mother left. A phrase Niccola had said, kept running through her mind, *we can only trust Jesus, hang onto His faith.*

'Yes!' Eliora shouted. *'Think about that, Bella. Think hard.'*

"Can I hang onto your faith, Yeshua? I just don't have enough faith. I have nothing left. This unbelief keeps coming back all the time." She stared into the darkness, her mind doing mental acrobatics as she thought it through. "Yes, I can hold on to your faith, Yeshua. Just like the woman who was sick for twelve years, held onto your robe and wouldn't let go. That was holding onto your faith, wasn't it? Arabella sat up in bed and turned on the bedside lamp. Reaching for her phone, she searched for that passage of scripture. Her lips moving as she read the passage, and at verse 48, her eyes opened in wonder as the truth cracked open the kernel of unbelief and dealt it a death blow. "Daughter, be of good comfort: thy faith hath made thee whole; go in peace," she whispered. "Oh!" She was startled. "Lord, if I hang onto your faith, your faith becomes my faith. Okay. Let's do this." Arabella closed her eyes, allowed her spirit to rise in faith and prayed. "Father, I am coming to you through the faith of Yeshua. I am using His faith. I ask that Saffie will be returned to us. But, even if she is in Heaven with you, then I know she is safe with you. I believe, though, because I have asked, that she will come home, and," Arabella dared to step further into faith, "I ask that she come home today. I believe through Yeshua's faith."

She turned her lamp off and lay back down, a huge smile on her face. Before drifting back to sleep, the last thing she heard was Yeshua telling her to hang on to Him in thanksgiving and praise. Her heart heard and responded. Her sleep was filled with the echoes of Angels worshipping, and her spirit and mind responded, joining in with them.

Though it had been a sleep-deprived night, Arabella woke with joy in the morning. A surety of faith had been birthed in her 2-o'clock vigil. All day, she kept praising God, and every time her faith took a hit, she firmly reminded her thoughts that she was holding onto Yeshua's faith. In the afternoon, with anticipation, she got off the school bus, looking forward to seeing her beloved cat. Pushing the front door of the house open, she called out, "Grandma, I'm home."

The answering call came, "Hello lovely girl."

Arabella hurriedly took her shoes off and ran into the kitchen, expectancy inscribed in all the planes of her face. "Is Saffie home?" she asked Evelyn, fully expecting to see the little cat.

"I'm sorry, Love. No, she isn't. I'm so sorry."

Arabella had been sure, so very sure that the cat

would have returned. As though her mind was a dartboard, the thoughts came swiftly, *See, it didn't work. You don't have enough faith. You failed because of your unbelief. You are a failure.*

Her Spirit immediately responded with Yeshua's words, "Thank me!"

Arabella took a deep breath, "We need to thank Him, Grandma. In everything, give thanks."

"Yes, you are absolutely right. Have your afternoon tea, and then you had better do your homework."

As Arabella went upstairs, she spoke her new mantra of "I WILL thank the Lord. I WILL give thanks in all things."

Determinedly, Arabella forced her mind to her homework, concentrating fiercely with her tongue between her lips as she fought and won with the maths.

They were a subdued family during dinner. For Joshua, who was often on the receiving end of grief when a pet died, it was especially poignant. He felt that he held his daughter's heart, and that was a responsibility he took to the Lord daily, especially at the moment.

Arabella didn't say much about her private struggle with belief and faith. It felt too new and too raw. She would save it for later.

There was no cajoling to do dishes that night. Her mother didn't have to ask; Arabella just did her chores, then excused herself for the evening. She wanted to be alone, to wrestle through this.

Eliora was excited. She knew where this was going. As Arabella sat in her prayer chair, Eliora deliberately caused Arabella to drop her Bible. Eliora quickly changed the pages to Job 5 verse 18.

Arabella reached down to pick the book up. Her glance landed on the scripture that Eliora had prepared. 'Blessed indeed is the man whom God corrects; so, do not despise the discipline of the Almighty. For He wounds, but He also binds; He strikes, but His hands also heal.' Her eyes darting from line to line. A dim light shone in her understanding, but it wasn't bright enough yet for her to see properly. The evening grew dark, and Arabella just sat in her chair, her mind roaming through all she had been taught, continually coming back to "In everything give thanks, for this is the will of God."

Yeshua stood by her chair. "Thank me," He said.

Arabella sat, unmoved.

"Come in thanksgiving, in everything give thanks. Hold onto my hand, Arabella."

The light in her heart grew a little brighter.

"My grace is sufficient for you, Arabella. Hold onto me."

Sighing, Arabella started talking to her friend Yeshua. The one who loved her so dearly. "Yeshua, it is through an act of my will that I am continuing to hold onto you. I don't have any faith left to believe that Saffie will come home. But you have all the faith I will ever need. So, Yeshua, I'm holding onto your faith." Her eyes started leaking tears down her face. "Yeshua, if Saffie isn't coming home, then I choose to trust you in that. I don't understand, but I choose you." She held her arms up. "I surrender to you, Lord."

The Angels in the room started applauding, clapping and cheering her. The victory was now assured.

Through the night, Arabella woke often, the barbs and taunts from the enemy continuing to mock her, mock her lack of faith. She acknowledged them all. "Yes. I don't have great faith. But I have as much faith as a little seed, and I combine my faith with Yeshua's faith. And He has a great big faith."

She slept again until her alarm roused her.

"I will praise you, Lord," she said as she got dressed. "I will trust you, Lord," she said as she went down the stairs. "I believe, Lord, my faith is in you."

A little voice spoke softly into her mind as she reached the bottom of the stairs.

'His mercies are renewed every morning.'

Arabella bowed her head, grateful for the refreshing dew of His love.

The still, small voice spoke again. *'Sorrow comes in the night, but joy comes in the morning.'*

Startled, as though just waking up, Arabella yelled, "Mum, Dad, Saffie is coming home today. God just told me." She ran into the kitchen where her father was nursing his coffee. "Dad, God just told me, 'Sorrow comes in the night, but joy comes in the morning.' Dad, I KNOW that Saffie is coming home today."

Joshua pulled his daughter into his loving father's arms and held her close. "You are such a blessing to us, my lovely girl." His eyes were wet as he released her. "Our Father God loves us so much. I'd better go to work, sweetheart. Let me know as soon as Saffie comes home."

"I will, Dad. Love you."

School was a nuisance to someone expecting a miracle. Eliora knew though that the timing of the Lord was always perfect.

The bus ride home that afternoon seemed to take as long as eternity, but when she finally got off, she ran inside, fully expecting to see her beloved cat.

Nothing.

Silently, Evelyn put her afternoon tea in front of her. Arabella ate and drank woodenly, simply serving her body's needs without appreciating the taste.

"Thanks, Grandma. I'll go and do my homework now." Arabella dragged herself up the stairs and into her room, dumping her school bag on the floor, and started to get out of her school clothes. As she turned to hang them up, her glance fell on her prayer chair. And her beloved cat. Saffron looked up at her with her Siamese cat smile, purring loudly.

Arabella dropped to the floor, just staring at the

precious gift on her chair. "Where did you come from? Oh, Saffie. Yeshua, thank you. THANK YOU!" she shouted.

Evelyn heard the shouting and ran up the stairs. "Bella, are you alright?" She ran into the girl's room and stopped. Her hand flew to her mouth. "Oh, dear Lord, Lord, thank you. Oh Father, thank you."

She walked across the bedroom, staring at the cat, her hand going to Arabella's head. "Where did she come from?"

"I don't know; she was just asleep here on my prayer chair. She has never slept on my prayer chair before. Oh, Grandma. Yeshua is so faithful."

In Heaven, the Angels cheered loudly. Yeshua smiled so widely that His face was radiant with joy and love.

"That's my girl," He said. "That's my Arabella. What a lioness she is becoming."

CHAPTER THIRTY-TWO

After Arabella's triumph over her doubts and unbelief, she started looking for opportunities to exercise her fledgling faith muscles. Her persistent discipline in her spiritual life had transferred into her study; her dream of serving her friends in India as a nurse, was coming steadily closer as she persisted in her schoolwork. Maths, biology and chemistry, she saw now, were part of God's creation, and that knowledge made the complexity far more interesting. When she looked at a chemical formula, instead of her mind boggling, Arabella saw the hand of God. For all she had learned, the times she had sat among the stars, it all made sense. The patterns were beautiful.

"Just like the puzzle of the Mazzaroth," she said as she tried to explain her new understanding to Evelyn.

Thus it was one night, when sleep claimed her mind and body but liberated her spirit, that Yeshua called her to come up higher.

He pulled the atmosphere across with His hand, and together they stepped through into what could have been a complex chemical formula. It was like a very busy roadway, more of a spaghetti junction, but instead of grey tarmac, the roads were made of light. Here, there, the roads glowed brightly. Everything connected by grids made of brilliantly golden threads. As Arabella looked around, she was aware of how three-dimensional it all was, and found herself travelling as light along these grids. However, some of them seemed to have parts missing, or the roads were dull and not brilliantly lit. They were separated from the flow and were not functioning properly. People, animals, creation, everything was affected by this separation. On the well-lit roads, people were busy, going up and down, fixing any broken places, and creating new roadways where there weren't any before.

Standing by the dim or missing roads were Angels. They weren't doing anything, just standing. To Arabella, it looked as though they were waiting.

Arabella looked at Yeshua. "What is this?" she asked Him.

"Watch," He said to her.

She turned her attention back to the buzz of activity, noticing how people and Angels worked together. Then, with a startled "OH!" she saw herself busy working on one part of a roadway. The 'other Arabella' began weaving the separated threads back into the grid with her light.

Yeshua laughed at the look on her face.

"What is this? How can I be there and here?" She leaned forward as though to see better. "Can I go and talk to myself? What is happening?"

Yeshua answered her, "The roads are the prayers of my people. Each one carries a unique song and spectrum of light. As narrow as a strand of hair, some prayers are joined with many others to form a larger stream or road. Other prayers are like great pipelines that have opened up wider pathways between heaven and earth. Look," He said, pointing at a large road that led downwards, far, far, far beyond where she could see. "Where the Angels are standing doing nothing, it is because no one is praying."

"But what about those roads that have holes in them. And why are the Angels just standing doing nothing?" Arabella's response carried a hint of frustration.

Yeshua looked at her. "The roads that have holes in them or where the lights are particularly dim, are where the people have stopped praying. And the people fixing those roads are those who are praying for others," He said. "Look," Yeshua pointed to where the other Arabella was working. Angels were working with her.

"This is what happens when you pray in my will for someone or something. Your prayers activate the Angels to work in those situations and create a new roadway or fix a damaged one. Every prayer carries light, frequency and sound. You, my people, have my light, and with that light, you are to co-create with light for all of humanity. Love always wins, Bella."

She began to examine some of the prayers that were written on the roadways. The sound of weeping and travail, whispering and shouting, began as a mere vague whisper, which grew in intensity. Arabella looked around to find the source. It seemed to be coming from the large pipeline which led down towards the earth.

Mixed in with the cacophony of distress was music and liturgy. All were mixed together in this heavenly place to become one sonic wave of prayer. Though it all seemed confusing and chaotic, by the time the sounds reached the top of the pipeline, the blending of these diverse prayers produced a recognisable and steady rhythm, like crashing waves. Arabella looked deeper into the noise. She could hear choruses of voices, ebbing and flowing like ocean waves. Children's voices and grandparents' voices, teenagers, businessmen, and single mothers. All cultures and strata of humanity, crying to the Lord.

"This is where I stand and listen to my people. I hear their cries. I hear their love, and it all blends into one." Yeshua said.

Startled, she turned to Yeshua. "There are people who are crying, and their prayers are being heard here, but they are of other religions. How is that possible?"

"Listen again, Arabella. Do not judge what you do not understand. Listen to what they are saying." Yeshua pointed at one particular woman, a Hindu.

Arabella listened carefully. She heard, "God, if

you are really there, please help me." The refrain was repeated over and over again by many from all over the world. Each time a person called, an Angel flew immediately to their side, orchestrating that a light bearer would find the person, and the light was passed on to the one who had called for help.

"This is my Kingdom being enforced on the earth. Don't judge what you don't understand," He said again. "I have sheep in other pastures that you do not know of. They are all looking for me, and I send my word to them. They then have to choose. Choose me and all I have stored up for them, or..." Yeshua's voice trailed off, and He shrugged sadly.

Arabella watched carefully, allowing all she had learned to be instilled deep into her mind, absorbing the scene in front of her, of what happens when people pray according to the will of God. "Lord, I need to pray for others more, don't I?" she said, not so much a question as a statement. "How can my prayers be more effective?"

"Stay hidden in me, Arabella. Know me, know my written word, all of it, and stay deep in the rest of my living water, which is a place of deep strengthening of heart, mind, body and soul. Many have tried to do my work but have failed to stand in my counsel and ask for Wisdom."

Yeshua kissed Arabella on the forehead. "Sleep well, precious Arabella. We will talk again very soon."

He nodded at Eliora, who carried Arabella back

to her sleep.

"The time of the Oil and the Wine is almost here," He said to the Angels in attendance.

They bowed before Almighty God.

CHAPTER THIRTY-THREE

Eliora stood right at the front of the Council room, next to the Twenty-Four Elders. As Arabella's principal Angel, she had that right. Behind them were an immense crowd of Angels, either participating or eager to hear the next phase in Arabella's training.

At the thump, thump, thump of a halberd sounding its warning - the King is coming in - the entire assemblage bowed low.

The aroma of the King's presence went before Him, causing praise to well up from all who were gathered in the room. Its beauty flowed over the top of the many heads, gliding and interlacing with varied words, sounds, notes, alighting on Yeshua's head as a crown. Their praise and adoration of the King created a fragrance of rich incense.

Yeshua looked at those in the Council Room. Their love for Him showed in every gesture, every breath. He, in return, poured His love out, flowing back to them like a river containing refreshing life.

There was a collective intake of breath as the Angels breathed in the life-giving love. It was always beautiful and restorative.

Yeshua smiled. He loved them all. All His creation. "Thank you for coming," He said, "Eliora, I want to honour you for all you have done for Arabella."

Eliora bowed her head to Him. She would do anything for her Lord.

"You have all been instrumental in ensuring that Arabella has come to this point. The training she has gone through has been intense. But there is more to come. She must now learn to use everything she has been taught. To do this, my Father will be allowing the evil one certain access to her life. Your job, as always, is to ensure that the evil one does not cross the boundaries that have been set. You have full authority to engage him in warfare should he try to go outside the set parameters.

"Arabella has been given an arsenal of weapons to use," Yeshua continued.

The Angels nodded, knowing that the Lord would have provided lavishly for His beloved.

"She has my name. The power of my name breaks every chain. And my blood. Nothing can stand before the blood which speaks through all eternity. She has the sword of the Lord and the power of the Word. And, she has my love, and my love always wins. Now she needs to learn how to use them. Eliora," He said, looking directly at Arabella's Angel, "Your input is needed. As always, she is your principal assignment."

Eliora nodded and bowed.

"Good, then we need to start work. Thank you for attending," Yeshua nodded His head to them and left the room.

❦

Arabella scratched her head absently as she worked through the pre-exam worksheet. She had amazed herself at how a natural aptitude towards mathematics had revealed itself. "It's all about attitude," her father had told her, and it appeared that he was correct.

Finally completing the paper, she took a deep breath and expelled it in an audible huff. She put her head back, feeling the cricks in her neck releasing, and stretched her arms. "Finished," she said, "And now for some exercise."

Changing into her running gear, she charged down the stairs calling for Toby. "Going for a run, Grandma," she yelled towards the general vicinity of the kitchen. "Back in about an hour."

With Toby jogging along behind her, his three legs easily keeping up with her two, Arabella ran to the park, doing a full circuit, feeling her heartbeat elevate. 'A good workout,' she thought to herself as she gradually slowed her pace. There weren't many people around; most of them had gone home to get dinner. She walked over to a park bench, which was partially hidden by trees. The Tuis were busy seeking nectar from the red flowers. It looked like a serene place.

"Come on, Toby. Let's sit down for a while." The dog started to follow her then suddenly stopped. He sat on the ground and whined. "What's the matter, boy?" Arabella looked with concern at the little dog. "I know, you are getting older, and you only have three legs, not four." She bent to pick him up. Toby growled. Arabella was bewildered. Toby had never behaved like this before. Something wasn't right. Her shoulders started to tighten. The back of her neck prickled.

Toby scrabbled to get out of her arms. She dropped him in astonishment. The dog snarled, darting around behind her. Arabella swung around to see a hunk of wood swinging down towards her. Instinctively, she put her arms up, defending her face from the wood about to land on her head. Toby latched onto the attacker's ankle, biting with all the viciousness in his little doggy body.

Stumbling, Arabella screamed.

Eliora was ready to intervene. Access had only been given this far. The evil one was not allowed to cross that line.

From deep inside Arabella, a rage pushed its way up, activating the God-gene in her mind and body.

Her blood pressure rose, causing a pounding in her ears, and the adrenaline gland released its power. "In the name of Yeshua, get out!" she yelled. To her ears, it sounded weak. Confidence grew. "In the name of Yeshua, I command you to leave. Get out. Go!"

The demon operating through the man hesitated.

Bewildered, her attacker's mouth fell open.

Emboldened by the man's uncertainty, Arabella took a step forward. She raised her bruised right arm and pointed at him. "Get out! I rebuke you, foul demon, in Yeshua's name."

Shrieking in pain, the demon stopped its attack. "The Name! The Name! No! Not the Name!" it screamed in torment, and the Angels commissioned for this moment chased after it, their swords ready to fight; now they had been given permission by way of that name of power.

The man turned and ran, dropping the piece of wood as he fled.

Toby ran after him, growling and barking as loudly as he could.

"Toby, come. Toby. Come back," Arabella called the dog, anxious lest the man harm her little companion.

As she saw him running back towards her, she fell on all fours, the adrenalin slowly subsiding. "Toby, oh Toby. Thank God you are okay." Arabella's arms and legs started to shake, her heart pounding hard as nausea washed over her.

"Oh, God. Oh, God. Yeshua, help me, please." Arabella fumbled for her phone, pausing as another wave of nausea threatened to overwhelm her. She blinked several times, clearing her sight sufficiently to be able to see the speed dial on the front screen of the phone.

"Bella," the sound of her father's voice broke the last remnants of her control.

"Daddy! Daddy, please help me," her voice croaked, splintering with shock. It was all she could do to get those words out. The explanation was halting, her mind unable to articulate clearly.

Joshua broke all speed restrictions, his instinct to protect his child overriding any laws of the land.

"Bella, Bella, where are you?" He yelled, running frantically towards the location she had described.

"Daddy! I'm here, Daddy."

The aftermath of the attack felt like confusion, muddling her mind. All she wanted to do was crawl into bed where it was safe. The police had come and taken the initial details: Time seemed interminable as she gave her account, again and again. The piece of wood was bagged for evidence. The police photographer took photos of the scene from every angle, as well as photos of Arabella's arms.

Joshua did not want to let Arabella leave his side. He felt that somehow, illogical though it was, that he had failed to protect his daughter.

"Sir," the detective got Joshua's attention, "I recommend you take her to the hospital for medical attention and have her arms x-rayed for any possible breaks. We have enough information for now but will visit her at home in the morning for a full statement. And just so you know," he said quietly, so Arabella couldn't hear, "There have been a few other cases of this sort of attack in this area. Please do not allow her to come to the park when there aren't many people around." He looked grim, "Not until we catch this person, anyway."

Joshua simply nodded. If someone had asked him, he wouldn't have been able to say what he was feeling; a mix of disbelief, shock, anger and numbness. "Sweetheart," he spoke very gently to his daughter. "We really should take you to Emergency and have you checked over."

Arabella nodded. She was beyond tired.

The emergency department ordeal was mercifully brief as few people were waiting to be seen. The x-rays showed no breaks, and the doctor advised Arabella to take the rest of the week off school. "The bruising will be intense," he said.

Niccola had left work immediately after Joshua had phoned her. While she waited for them at home, she sat, then stood, pacing, sitting back down again, anxiously waiting. "I should have gone to the park," she said to Evelyn. Evelyn absently patted Niccola's arm.

It all felt surreal. This should not have happened. Like a thousand biting insects whining around her head, Evelyn's mind stumbled over the events before the attack. Should she have demanded Arabella stay home? Could she have stopped it? Logic told her mind there was nothing different she could have done. Her heart demanded recompense from the enemy.

Evelyn's lips were white. "They won't be much longer. Josh told you it's best you stay here. Bella will need you when they get home. In fact, I think that's them now," as she heard the garage door opening.

As soon as Arabella saw her mother, reaction hit hard. A thin wail from the depths of her emotions startled itself into a shrill sob. "Mummy," the inner child called for the security of mother. Her knees buckled.

Joshua picked her up and carried her into the lounge room, laying her on the couch.

Niccola sat on the floor by the couch, smoothing her daughter's hair back, running the back of her hand softly over Arabella's cheek. "Ssh, baby. Ssh. You are safe now. Safe at home." The soft tender words, fluttered their way into Arabella's heart, recapturing childhood security.

The family knit tighter than before over the evening meal that night. The profound sense of gratitude transferred from Arabella's safety to the blessing of the food before them.

Joshua prayed, "I ask you, Lord, to repay the attack twofold for causing fear in my child, and to remove the fear and its footholds in her soul and mind, and infuse courage and strength into her spirit. But I also ask that you seek out that man, and bring him to know Yeshua. Lord, I forgive him for what he did to my daughter."

"Amen," Niccola said.

"Amen," Evelyn echoed.

There was no prayer chair for Arabella that night. Lying in bed, watched over by her parents, Grandma Evelyn, and many Angels, Arabella eventually slept. Toby remained en garde. No one was going to harm anyone in his pack.

Yeshua sat on her bed. His hand caressed her long dark hair. "Beloved," He said, "I am so proud of you."

"And you also, Eliora," He commended the Angel.

"Yeshua?" Arabella's sleepy mind registered His presence. Her spirit was instantly alert. "I'm so glad you are here. I had such a fright."

The King looked stern. "Yes, you did. We are in a constant war, but you did so well, my daughter. I'm very proud of you."

"I did?" She asked Him, "I was so afraid. It was Toby that saw him off."

The Lord smiled at the dog, who wagged his tail fiercely, pride in his little doggy heart at fulfilling his duty.

"Yes, Toby has a brave heart. But what really saved you, Arabella, was one of your most powerful weapons."

She looked at Him in surprise. "I didn't have any weapons with me." To her, it was a simple statement.

"Oh, but you did, and furthermore, you used that weapon very well. Do you want to see what happened?"

Arabella nodded.

Yeshua parted time, so they were looking at the attack again. This time, Arabella saw it in multi-dimensional form. She saw the brutal heart of the man, the demon that held him and fed his brutality. But she also saw as her words, 'in the name of Yeshua,' were spoken, swords flew out of her mouth; the demon trembled, paused; the man was spooked. And she used that weapon again, stronger this time, with more power: 'In the name of Yeshua.' The demons fled, leaving the man discombobulated and confused. The power feeding him was gone. Shock waves rippled throughout all realms and dimensions.

Arabella's eyes widened. "Oh!" was all she could say.

The Lord laughed. "A VERY powerful weapon indeed," He said, "Well done, my beloved." He stroked her hair again, kissing her on the forehead, and smiled with great love as she slipped back into a deep, restful sleep.

The next day felt gentle after the jagged horror of the previous afternoon.

Niccola took the day off work, sitting with Arabella when the detective came to take a full written statement, seeking out minute details that might help in finding the perpetrator. "We take this very seriously," he said, "The charge against the perpetrator will probably be Assault with intent to injure or, at the very least, Assault with a weapon." He scribbled in his notebook.

Arabella looked at the notebook curiously. "I thought that sort of thing was only on TV," she said.

Niccola blinked tears away. Her daughter's sense of humour and curiosity was emerging again.

The police photographer took multiple photographs of her injuries, aiming her camera at every part of Arabella's arms, capturing many angles of where the wood had hit.

The police finished with their statement taking and photographing. It seemed as they left that the house sighed with relief.

Evelyn quietly got the three of them lunch, and Arabella went upstairs to rest.

Safiyya and her parents visited after dinner, enveloping the family with understanding love, born out of their own tragedies.

Niccola went back to work the following day, leaving Evelyn to watch over Arabella.

A quiet, soft morning; gentleness flowing from Yeshua through Evelyn.

As Arabella's mind uncurled from horror, Evelyn watched and waited for the right time. "My sweet, we need to deal with the trauma. If trauma gets its grip on you, it is very difficult to shift on later. Shall we do that?"

"I hadn't really thought about it, but yes, of course." Arabella quietened her mind and her heart, searching for Yeshua, looking through the eyes of her spirit.

Evelyn put her hand on Arabella's head. "Yeshua, I ask for your Blood over Arabella. In the name of Yeshua, I rebuke all trauma from the attack on Arabella. With the blood of Yeshua, trauma, I cut off your tentacles and declare that you have no place here. I cover Arabella with the Blood of Yeshua and remind her heart of the great love of God."

Sitting there listening to Evelyn take authority over the trauma, Arabella suddenly realised that she *had* been carrying trauma. If it weren't dealt with, it would affect her into her future. Bringing her mind into alignment with the mind of Yeshua, Arabella reached for His hand. Quietly, she commanded the trauma to leave her body. Waiting, revelling in the beauty of His presence, she felt the deliverance of the Lord fall on her.

Angels of healing ministered. The restorative blessing of love flowed around her, and trauma fell off, dissipating and vanishing. Arabella's shoulders slumped as the fear she had been carrying, reacted to the presence of Yeshua, and left.

Evelyn spoke scripture over Arabella. He shall preserve you from all evil and preserve your soul. He is your keeper, your shade at your right hand, for now and evermore!

Arabella felt as though the thick restrictive skin she had been wearing since the time of the attack had simply gone. She felt light, free, as though she could float away.

Joy came alongside her, beckoning to Eliora, who started to tickle Arabella using one of her wing feathers. Joy released the oil of gladness all through the house. Any residue of pain, terror and fear fled.

"Be well and thrive, Arabella," Joy declared, leaving her presence behind in the heart of both Arabella and Evelyn.

The Angels in the room bowed as the Spirit of Joy left.

"Grandma, thank you," Arabella hugged Evelyn. "I feel clean and free again."

Tears ran through the wrinkles on Evelyn's face. Her heart was full. The fruits of the Spirit danced around and through her. She brushed the tears off her face as Eliora caught them in her crystal vase to transfer to the pool of tears in Heaven.

"Let's go out for coffee now, Grandma," Arabella stood up, "I need to get out of the house."

Over the next few days, Arabella admired the yellow, purple and green-tinged bruising even though the healing bruises ached. While her body was bruised, her spirit wasn't.

Finally, the weekend came, when the family could sit together without the rush of work and general busyness. On Saturday morning, Joshua asked Arabella to go out for a drive with both him and Niccola.

"Where to?" she asked.

"Oh, just around. I just feel like driving," he said.

Niccola grinned.

"What?!" Arabella demanded. "What's going on?"

Joshua broke across her queries. "Ice-cream. Who wants ice cream?" He kept driving, leaving the familiar roads, and entering a more industrial looking area.

"There isn't any ice cream here, Dad. What are you doing?" Sitting in the backseat of the car, Arabella was curious and a little perplexed.

Joshua pulled into a car sales yard. "I just have to go and talk to a man about a dog," he said, getting out of the car.

Arabella didn't think anything of that. After all, it was probably one of her father's patients. She stared out the window, not looking at anything in particular, and was startled out of her reverie as her father opened the car door.

"Bella, come and have a look at this. I think you will just love this little girl," He said mischievously.

"A dog? Okay, then." She wasn't interested in someone else's dog, but as the man was standing there looking at her, she couldn't very well decline. "Hi," she said to the man, "What's your dog's name?"

The man looked confused. "I don't have a dog," he said.

Joshua gently pushed Arabella forward before

she could ask any further questions.

Niccola got out of the car and came over.

"Dad, what are you doing? You said you were going to talk to the man about a dog. He doesn't have a dog." She was getting bewildered and a little annoyed.

"This is what I want you to see, Bella." Joshua put his hand on the hood of a little blue car. "Mum and I are buying you a car for your birthday. You will be 17 very soon. You need a little more independence."

Standing with her mouth open, Arabella was unable to respond, completely stunned and in shock. "For me?" her voice squeaked, "You mean, I will have my own car?"

"Yes, you will have your own car, Bells. Mum and I were exploring ways to help you keep safe after the attack."

"Oh, Daddy, Mum. Thank you so much!" Arabella touched the car, feeling the cool metal under the sky-blue paint. "Can I get in it?" she asked the salesman, who hurried to open the door for her.

Joshua had a huge grin on his face. Niccola was just as excited. "I'll just go and do the paperwork, and then we WILL go and have an ice cream. Mum will drive your car home first."

"I'm going home with Mum," Arabella announced.

Later, much later, after the excitement of the car; after showing Evelyn the car; after ice cream;

after Arabella phoning Safiyya and telling her about her new blue car; finally, the family sat down together.

Niccola steered the conversation. "Dad and I talked about the incident in the park. Obviously, it's not safe for you to exercise in the park. And in view of the attack last week, it's time you gained a little more independence and went to the gym instead of running around a park. When you have your licence, you can drive yourself to the gym. We have paid for the car. It's not new; it would be foolish buying a new car for a learner driver," Niccola laughed wryly. "We will pay for your insurance until you finish university and have a job. Then it is your responsibility. I have booked your first driving lesson for next week. We expect you to obey the road code. This is your combined Christmas and birthday gift. Yes, it cost a lot, but you are worth so much more than any car. Love you, Bella darling," Niccola was teary-eyed.

"Thank you. Thank you so much. I love you both so much." There were no words that Arabella could find to describe her emotions." She reached over and scratched Toby's ears. "I need to go and find my prayer chair again. It feels like it's been a year, not just a few days." She looked ruefully at the fading bruises on her arms. "Thank you again."

Arabella found it difficult to stop her thoughts from wandering. Her Bible was open on her lap, but her gaze rambled from the window to the bed, to the Bible and off into the distance.

She watched the sun set. The purple flowers of the Jacaranda tree were edged with crimson light, casting shadows and staining the grass in scarlet and shadow.

Sighing deeply, Arabella tried again to focus her mind on Yeshua.

"Rest, Beloved," the small voice in her heart reminded her that though she might not be able to enter into the deep place with Yeshua, He was constantly with her.

"Yeshua, thank you," Arabella breathed in deeply and controlled the breath out. Her shoulders relaxed. Closing her eyes, she envisioned Yeshua standing by her. "I so long to be with you, Lord, to be able to actually see you with my eyes."

The levee holding back the horror of the attack, cracked. Fear held tightly in her heart, poked its finger through the crack, widening it. Waters of panic ran rivulets through the rift, widening it further, until the breach gave way completely. Arabella cried, reaction finally setting in.

Eliora took every tear and stored them carefully in the crystal vial until she could empty it into the Pool of Tears.

"Good," Yeshua said.

Stunned, Arabella looked at Him. "What do you mean 'good'? I shouldn't be crying. That's not being brave."

"Oh, dear," Yeshua said, "No one told me that I shouldn't cry when I was on earth. I cried over

Jerusalem, and I cried when my friend Lazarus died. My Father designed you to cry, Arabella. Because if you do not cry, it causes your heart to harden. So, cry, my beloved. Cry until the pain is released, and my Spirit fills up the empty place."

He held her as she sobbed, sobs gradually easing to the occasional hiccup.

"Why didn't you protect me, Yeshua? You said you would never leave me. Why didn't you stop that man?"

"Didn't you see me there, Bella? Didn't you see that man hit me? When he hit you, he hit me, too. Mankind has free will. They can use it for good or for evil. That man chose evil." Yeshua looked at her calmly. "There are many things you have yet to learn. The evil one has desired to sift you, Arabella. He sees who you are and tries to destroy you. But you have my name. You have my Blood. You have my love. You have your weapons which you must learn to use."

"I don't feel that I did very well, Lord. Shouldn't I have been able to talk to him and tell him about you?"

"You must learn to see with the eyes of the Spirit, Arabella. All is not as it seems on the surface. This world is a mere reflection of the reality of the spirit realm. What you saw was a man with evil in his heart. What you did not see was the evil behind the man, tormenting him."

She remembered her night visions, where Yeshua showed her what had happened, and nodded.

"Yes, that's true," she replied.

"For as long as you are on this earth, there will be trials. You will face temptations, and sometimes, evil may seek you out. It is then that the weapons you hold become most powerful."

Arabella caught the meaning of the words, even if she didn't fully understand all that Yeshua said.

"You must rest now, Beloved. Your mind, heart and body need to heal. I will never leave you."

Arabella stood up, stretched and yawned. "Yes, I do need to rest. Shower, and then bed for me."

As she lay in the dark, thinking through her conversation with Yeshua, she reflected that she had a lot to think about and learn. It wasn't that she hadn't heard of these things before; it was that He put them to her in a different way; a way that opened up the ways of the Spirit of God.

Toby jumped onto the bed. He had appointed himself Arabella's guardian. Eliora stroked him, and the little dog drifted off to sleep, as did his mistress.

CHAPTER THIRTY-FOUR

Study, study, study. If it wasn't school work, it was learning to drive. One was sometimes laborious, the other exciting. With summer passing rapidly, the spectre of her final year of school sent butterflies flapping wildly through Arabella's tummy.

Paediatric nursing was at the forefront of her mind, sharpening her focus, and alongside that, was her friend Lauren. Now she was older, Arabella understood better what caused Lauren's disabilities.

"But Lord," she queried aloud, tapping her front teeth with her pen. "Why haven't you healed Lauren?"

She heard the Lord chuckle. "Why haven't YOU healed Lauren?" He answered.

"ME! But you are the healer, not me."

"Arabella. Have you not yet learned? In me, you live, you move, you have everything there is. I have given to you all power, all authority, under Heaven and in the earth. Why haven't YOU exercised YOUR authority?" Yeshua looked at her sternly. "I have given you weapons; the power of my name, the power of my blood, the power of faith. You have free access to everything my Father has given me. WHY are my people not using their authority?"

Arabella was shocked. Everything she had believed regarding healing was undone in one conversation. "But Lord, I thought we had to ask you to heal people?"

Yeshua answered her with a scripture. "Mark 16 verse 17 to 18."

She quickly pushed her schoolwork aside and opened her Bible.

'And these signs will accompany those who believe: In My name, they will drive out demons; they will speak in new tongues; they will pick up snakes with their hands, and if they drink any deadly poison, it will not harm them; they will lay their hands on the sick, and they will be made well.'

"Tell me where it says that you have to beg me to do anything?" Yeshua spoke very firmly.

Arabella got up and went to look out the window. Her mind was like crazy spinning wheels, thoughts tumbling, disjointed, and chaotic.

Yeshua waited. He had waited 2000 years for His people to wake up, like a slow rumbling age. He stood tall as the frequency of His blood shattered the lies of the enemy, blasting apart control and misinformation, starting Arabella on the journey to freedom.

She turned to face Him. "So, what you are saying, is that what we have been taught is basically a dilution of the truth. That if I am in you, and you are in me, then we have complete access to everything you have given us?"

"That's exactly what I'm saying," Yeshua responded. "You have access to my Father through me. You have access to Heaven, you have access to deliverance, healing, being transported in my Spirit to another place, you have access to EVERYTHING. There is nothing that I have kept from you. My love always wins."

Shocked, Arabella sat down again.

"It all comes back to unbelief, Arabella. My people have been taught systems and religion, not truth. For centuries, they have been taught that only the Priest or Minister has any authority, and they have to come to me through a man, with confession, or as though the Minister somehow knows me better than they do. Lies." He spoke with such anger that Arabella was astonished.

"The enemy has sought to make my people completely powerless, and destroy them. But I say, as of today, that my truth will be taught and my people will be set free." Yeshua's face softened, and He spoke more gently. "Remember, I in you, and you in me. Just as I prayed: 'Father, I have given them the glory You gave Me, so that they may be one as We are one— I in them and You in Me— that they may be perfectly united, so that the world may know that You sent Me and have loved them just as You have loved Me.'" Yeshua started to pace. "I have given you the glory my Father gave me, Arabella. Do you understand now?"

She nodded. "Yes, I think so."

He smiled at her, "It is written. I only do what I see the Father doing. Whatever the Father does, so I also do."

The vision faded.

Arabella stared at where Yeshua had been standing. What just happened? This encounter was outside of the normal parameters of her understanding.

Over the next few days, her mind grappled with what Yeshua had revealed, and as she studied the scriptures quoted, she saw just how deluded she and the church had been, for it was exactly as He had said.

Yeshua watched Arabella wrestling with Truth. He sent Understanding to her, and as Arabella studied the scriptures, Understanding poured Truth into her mind. Truth and Understanding stood united, pushing against the boundaries of lies that had been taught to the Church and by the church authorities. As Arabella sought to know what was real and what shadows she had believed, Truth spoke through the written Word of God. Understanding took the veil off Arabella's mind and eyes.

Arabella always knew she could ask Evelyn, and if Evelyn didn't know, they would pray together, research, until they had their answers.

"There is one simple way to grow into this truth, Love," Evelyn said, "And that is to simply do it. Just do exactly as the Bible says to do. Yeshua said it, you believe it, end of story."

Sunday seemed an interminable time away. Arabella was ferocious in holding onto the truth she had been shown, and she knew just who she was going to pray for: Lauren. Arabella had questioned Yeshua about why Lauren wasn't healed, and He had told her: *'because you, Arabella, haven't healed her.'*

"I'm going to fast this weekend," Arabella told her parents after dinner on Friday night. "I have something I need to pray about."

Niccola had looked at her daughter over the top of her reading glasses and simply said, "Okay."

Joshua's eyebrows rose so high they caused the lines on his forehead to become deep creases.

Arabella pulled away from everyone for that time. There was a need, deep inside, to be alone. She went for walks with Toby, spent time in her bedroom, and rescheduled her driving lesson to coincide with Saturday night's meal.

The inner stillness remained with her as she walked into church on Sunday morning. Looking for a quiet place where she and Lauren could be private, she found Lauren where she usually sat.

"Lauren, I want to pray for you," Arabella had no preamble, no social niceties. The need to declare Lauren's healing was intense.

Looking a bit startled at such a blunt approach, Lauren gave a little laugh and said, "Well, hello to you, too, Arabella. I would love you to pray for me."

"Sorry, I was a bit abrupt, but I really need to pray for you. Could we go into the side room? It's a bit more private there."

"Sure, okay then. Can you please help me get up?" Lauren reached for her walking stick with one hand, putting her other hand out for Arabella to help steady her as she got up. "All right then, Bells, so what's this about then?"

Arabella slowly guided Lauren towards the side room, shutting the door behind them.

Lauren looked a little surprised but amiably took the seat offered.

"I want to pray for you, Lauren. I've been talking to Jesus - Yeshua and asking Him why He hasn't healed you. He told me off. He asked why I hadn't healed you because He has already given me authority in His name to heal you. So that's what I'm going to do."

Arabella took a deep breath. She saw Yeshua as He was, inside her. She saw herself inside of Jesus. Gently, Arabella put her hand on Lauren's head. "In the name of Yeshua, Lauren, I command all the damaged neural pathways in the damaged basal ganglia in your brain be rewired and healed, and all movement within your body to be completely restored. I command life into all parts of your body, Lauren."

The words of life were heard in the frequency of Lauren's body. All the neural pathways lit up and vibrated to the name of Yeshua. Lightning seemed to hit at points along the brain's circuit board, with long-dead synapses flickering, fluttering.

Lauren's spirit heard the sound of life, the strongest frequency of the Name above all names. Her spirit called to her mind to accept Truth, and her mind and soul commanded her brain to alter the physical field of atoms in her brain.

Pure faith stood against unbelief. The King honoured His name. The universe responded, and Lauren's brain began to rewire itself, finding new neural pathways, reactivating those long dead.

The words formed themselves in Arabella's mouth, and she spoke them loudly, "Light be."

An explosion of pure light hit the middle of Lauren's dead Basal Ganglia, triggering reactions along all the synapses and pathways of the brain. Tiny dots of light, like tiny nuclear reactors, travelled at speed faster than light: restoring, rewiring and renewing.

Lauren jerked as though hit by electric voltage. Her muscles started to respond to the orders from the brain, with the leg reacting first.

"Bella, Oh, Bella, look! Thank you, Jesus. Oh, thank you, Yeshua." Lauren struggled to her feet, not even realising that her speech was also improving. "Bella! Arrrghh! Oh my gosh! Bella, I can feel it happening."

Yeshua laughed. The Angels in the room joined hands and started dancing around Lauren and Arabella.

A stillness and absolute certainty of Lauren's healing settled over Arabella. Then she started to giggle. And laugh, and when someone passing by the room heard the laughter and opened the door, they were astounded to see Lauren standing without her walking-stick, laughing with Arabella.

"Yeshua has healed me," was Lauren's profound statement of faith.

Over the following weeks and months, Arabella watched with giddy joy as her friend started regaining function in the once useless limbs, and her speech was gradually restored.

During a prayer-chair time, Arabella had an important question to ask. "Yeshua, why wasn't Lauren healed instantly? Why is it taking so long?"

"Often, the person who needs healing must be healed in their heart and mind first," Yeshua replied. "Many times, when someone is sick, it is because they have believed lies or are holding onto things that are actually killing them. Unforgiveness and bitterness will destroy a person. So, for Lauren, I am healing her heart and mind, and as she allows me to heal those, then her body is also responding. Lauren is even now being healed, and she will come into perfect health, for she will overcome by my blood and by the word of her testimony."

Arabella nodded. "That makes perfect sense. I get that. Thank you."

※

As the months passed, Arabella sat her driving test and passed.

Evelyn was grateful to no longer have to chauffeur Arabella everywhere but also sad. The child was gone, and the young woman emerged. The greatest joy though, were the times when she and Arabella would journey in the things of God together.

"Just think," Evelyn said to Christina and Angela, "I thought I was coming to be a Grandma to a young girl, and now that young girl is almost grown. It won't be long before she no longer needs me."

The year felt as though it was rushing past, with the final school exams drawing closer.

"Have you thought about which university you want to study at?" Joshua asked one evening. "Mum and I have been researching the best university for your nursing degree, and we have found that the one in Aunt Bronnie's city has the best reputation. What about if you lived with her for that time?"

"I need to pray about that," Arabella said. "But it sounds like a good plan. I'm going upstairs."

As she bounded up the stairs, the vitality of youth still on her side, her mind was quickly sorting through her options, what it would mean to live with Aunt Bronnie; Would she be able to find a church that truly believed what Yeshua taught. *I'll call Safiyya*, she decided.

No conversation with her friend was ever short, but at least she knew she could talk things through and that Safiyya would pray if she said she would.

Arabella was not prepared for Safiyya's response. "You know I was going to do accounting," she said, "But, I have changed my mind. When the conflict in Syria is over, my country will need qualified medical people. I am going to study nursing. My father also researched which university I should study at, and he said the same as your father. Maybe we could both stay with Aunt Bronnie?"

For Niccola and Joshua, to have Safiyya go to the same university with their beloved daughter, took the weight of anxiety off them. Bronnie, of course, was in agreement and, in her usual delighted way, declared the household of three girls would be party central. Arabella laughed. She remembered the shopping trips, where Bronnie had to sit down for coffee every few hours. There was no way Bronnie would be able to keep up with a party-central lifestyle.

દે ∽

Exams!

There was enormous pressure to achieve. With her application to the university accepted subject to her exam results, Arabella felt stressed, very stressed. But she felt she had been diligent in her study, learning, and understanding, and now the exams were here, there was nothing more she could do except pray.

Her prayer-chair time was even more important now than it had ever been before. It was strength for the next day, refreshing her mind, soul and spirit. It was like standing under the clearest waterfall that washed all dirt away and refreshed every molecule.

Even while Arabella tried to keep all other thoughts banished until after her exams, something had been growing in intensity and now could not be ignored. She noticed that her church, along with many other churches, had been growing cold over the last few years. No passion for Yeshua, no collaboration with Heaven. There were a lot of good works, a lot of reaching out to the community. But it all seemed to simply be to appear acceptable, so that people wouldn't feel threatened when they came to church. The glory of the ardent praise for God had subsided into singing songs.

"Lord, why is that? People were so surprised when I did as you said and commanded Lauren to be healed. They all wanted *me* to heal them. Why can't they go to you for their own healing? Why me, Lord? What has happened? As I look around,

I see a lot of people saying they are Christians, but I can't see their light."

Grumpily, Arabella tried to order her thoughts into alignment with the mind of Christ.

"Aarrghh!" she exclaimed. "Lord, I'm sorry, but I'm rather worked up over this. Where is the power in the church? Why do so many seem to be content to just take a smooth ride through life. How can they not long for you, crave your presence! They say they know you, but do they, really? If they did, surely they wouldn't be happy to just cruise along."

Irritated with herself, with what she was observing, Arabella closed her books. She had a study day tomorrow. She'd done enough tonight, and now she just wanted to shower and go to bed.

In a dream, in a vision of the night, when deep sleep fell, Yeshua came for Arabella.

"You have asked me many questions about my church," He said. "It was me who caused you to see what is happening so clearly. Now is the time when you will step into what you were born for. All you have been trained for is coalescing in this moment."

Arabella looked around her. She seemed to be hovering over the earth. She could see its curvature, and everywhere she looked, there was some light. On the beautiful green and blue planet, sometimes solitary lights shone brightly in places of great darkness. Some places seemed to have intense clusters of light. As she looked further, she could see that some of the light was very dim, flickering as though it was ready to go out.

She looked to Yeshua for an explanation.

"The lights you see are those who carry my light. In the very dark places where there are only a few lights, notice how those lights shine the brightest. And then look again," Yeshua pointed to the dim lights. "See here? They have comfort, they have all they need, but they are asleep. If they ever knew who they were, they have forgotten and are sitting in church pews, fast asleep. It is time for the Church to remember whose they are. Are you ready?" He looked at Arabella.

"I think so. But I'm only me, Lord; I'm only one person."

"Are you, really?" Yeshua said drily, "You will be surprised."

In the place between places, outside of time, in the place where Christ is King, Yeshua called loudly.

"Wake up, Church," Yeshua snapped His fingers, commanding life into the sleeping people. "It is time to awaken. It is now Kingdom time."

Arabella stood in the middle of the space of no time. She raised her arms to the Lord in praise and thanksgiving, declaring the words of life before all the spiritual authorities.

"WE ARE
THE GOVERNMENT OF LIGHT;
WE ARE

THE LIVING LIGHT LAWS."

Overhead, from the Father's throne, bolts of lightning shattered time, severing links from man's corruption to the purity of His Son. Thunder rolled, crashing against the plans of the evil one and shattering them to nothing but shards. All the evil plans in mankind's hearts were shown openly, exposed, and the corruption in the world stood naked.

Arabella looked and reached for her Father in Heaven. She felt the power of His great love course through her being. It swelled, gaining strength, giving life to every particle in her Spirit being. Her mouth filled with power, her tongue felt as though it swelled, filling itself with the power from the Throne.

Yeshua changed and became a mighty lion. The lion opened His mouth and ROARED.

As the roar reverberated, bronze ceilings of control began to shatter.

Arabella caught the roar and unleashed the power in her mouth, roaring the letters of her name, Lion, Ara, אֲרָי.

"Ara, Ara, Ara," she called, like a smaller lion sounding its name - Ara אֲרָי. And again "Ara, Ara, Ara."

From not too far away came answering roars from other lions, "Ara, Ara, Ara,"

And then further away again, and on, on, on, the roars of Ara, Ara, Ara, echoed, sounding faintly, resounding around the planet known as

Earth.

Ara, Ara, Ara, Ara, Ara, Ara, Ara, Ara, Ara, Ara, Ara, Ara.

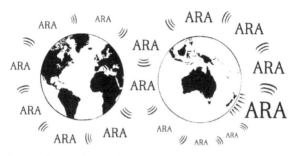

Ara, Ara, Ara, reverberating and answering from around the world, many lions calling, echoing faintly out of hearing and coming back faintly Ara, Ara, Ara, Ara, then sounding louder, Arabella's roar joining with the many others.

Yeshua, the mighty King of all kings, stood clothed with the rainbow from around the throne, drew His sword and slew a mighty grotesque being. The great cloud of confusion that blinded the hearts of mankind, trembled for a moment and then shattered. Dream spells, scrambling curses, religion, not truth echoing through space and time, were utterly destroyed.

"REARRANGE THE LIVING LETTERS!" Yeshua shouted, "It is release time for my people."

The spicy fragrance from the prayers of the Saints hung like a heavy cloud around Yeshua. His longing for the restoration of His people, their deep desire to find the Father amid great trials. The undercurrents of prayer-steady waves of love, compassion, desperation, and hope that ebbed and flowed as the prayers ascended.

"IT IS TIME!" He shouted.

Arabella stood with her sword raised in one hand and the living word of God in the other. The power of God in her mouth, poured out, "We have overcome, by the Blood of the Lamb, and the word of our testimony."

Yeshua called His little lions to arc with each other. Around the world, they touched their swords, one to another to another. As the encircling was complete, Yeshua blew on their swords, life-giving breath.

Holy Spirit's whirlwind ran faster and faster around Earth; larger, farther and widening circles, encompassing universes and all solar systems. Trembling, space, touching all in its path. Faster and faster, ripples in time rolling up and unfolding into a new timeline moment.

Arabella turned and turned again, her sword flashing, the God-breathed authority in it combining with Yeshua and her fellow believers. Wrinkles in history being smoothed and born again.

Lightning flashed through time, expanding, decreasing, renewing. And all was suddenly still.

The Sons of God watched as Yeshua reached one hand to the future and the other to the past, pulling them together. He smiled, love pulsating from before the past to beyond the future, and the Sons bore witness to the future of mankind, taken back to Eden, back to the original purpose.

"So, it begins," He said.

Arabella suddenly woke up. It was dark, not yet dawn. Her mouth still felt full, residual power remaining in her. But all she had witnessed in her night vision stayed fresh in her mind.

"Lord!" was all she could say.

"This wasn't a dream, Arabella," the Lord said very clearly to her. "This is the beginning, of the beginning."

CHAPTER THIRTY-FIVE

Arabella did her best to describe her night-time adventure with the Lord to her parents and Evelyn. Her parents nodded, not fully understanding, but Evelyn caught it immediately.

"Restore my Mazzaroth." Evelyn's words were full of wonder. "It has begun. That I would have lived to have seen this happen. Lord God, I praise you."

Arabella smiled. She understood what Evelyn was saying. "The great shaking has started. Nothing will ever be the same again." She laughed ruefully. "It almost seems like a waste of time. Except I know I'm supposed to study nursing; therefore I shall. After all, none of us know God's time frame, do we?" She stretched, yawning widely. "Right, I have my last exam tomorrow, so I need to get my head into that space. Love you all," she said as she headed upstairs.

The next day, after her final exam, Arabella took the school bus for the last time. For the last time, she dumped her school bag down, and for the last time as a school girl, took her afternoon tea with

Evelyn. "It feels weird, Grandma." The focal point of study and exams had collapsed. All that lay in its place was summer, and then she and Safiyya would make the long drive to start their new life at university.

Evelyn nodded. She understood, for wasn't that precisely what she had felt all those years ago when she had first come to live with this beloved family? "I guess that leaves me in decision time as well, doesn't it?"

"What do you mean?" Arabella looked surprised.

"Well, I can't stay here forever, can I, Love. Once you are gone to university, you no longer need me to be here for you."

"But this is your home, Grandma." Arabella was disconcerted.

"Yes, sweetheart, it has been my home, and I have been so very happy here with you, but I am getting older, as well. I think that it's time to do as my children wanted me to do after David died and go to live near them." Her eyes filled with tears. "I am so very proud of you, Bella. Very proud. You are a beautiful young woman. I know that whatever you set your mind to do, you will achieve it because you know who your God is. You know where your strength comes from."

As Christmas came closer, Arabella and Safiyya spent more time together, the freedom of summer days beckoning. The days seemed frivolous, never-ending, celebrations of life and Arabella's eighteenth birthday.

Despite reassurances from Joshua and Niccola, Evelyn had come to a decision; to sell her home, pack everything up, and live near her children.

It truly was the end of an era.

She felt she had done all that the Lord had asked her to, and even though she would be gone from Arabella's day-to-day life, Arabella would never be gone from Evelyn's heart.

The day came when Evelyn drove away from what had been her home for six years. Janel rode inside Evelyn's car. Her new assignment would be just as challenging as the last: new season, new assignment.

Arabella felt bereft. She wandered through Grandma's cottage, now empty of everything that held the memories of Evelyn. She knew though, just as her mother had said, that she would get used to Grandma not being there, and after-all, things were about to change forever when she left for university.

Safiyya and Arabella made the most of the time they had left, visiting friends, shopping and starting to pack up for their three-year degree. The two families spent Christmas together, with Safiyya very grateful that her parents would have Joshua and Niccola as friends when both girls left in just a few weeks.

Finally. Day zero.

Arabella's little car was packed full of much-needed girl things: suitcases of clothes, goodies for snacks on the long drive, books.

Joshua rolled his eyes as he watched Arabella trying to fit just one more bag into the car. "Girls," he muttered.

Niccola playfully punched him on the arm. "She's young; she'll learn after she's done it a few times."

"Right girls, you need to leave now if you are going to catch the ferry. Let's pray, and then you have to go," Orhan spoke up decisively. He hated saying goodbye to his daughter, but secretly, he was looking forward to having Rana to himself. "Just like a honeymoon again," he had whispered to her.

Orhan prayed. He spoke from his place as one with authority, as Safiyya's father. He declared safety over the girls and called on their Angels to protect them. The collective prayers of four parents over their two daughters wielded power in the spirit realm. The Angels heard the word of the Lord for safety and obeyed.

Arabella started the car. Solemn, somewhat scared but excited faces from the girls, and forced smiling faces from the parents. There would be a few tears that night from the mothers.

"Eliora," Yeshua said. "Arabella and Safiyya need to experience my goodness, so there will be no doubt at all that I am with them."

The Angel bowed to the Lord, receiving her instructions.

"What time is the ferry crossing booked for?" Safiyya was checking the GPS on her phone. "Do we have time to stop for something to eat?"

"Of course. I've left plenty of time! And I don't even need to speed." Arabella laughed with the carefree attitude of the young.

"Good," Safiyya said, "Because I desperately need the bathroom."

"Have a look and see where the nearest cafe is. We'll stop there."

"Uh," Safiyya was checking online, "Oh, it's only a few minutes away."

It was with relief that Arabella turned the car off. She had never driven that far before and was getting tired. Coffee and something to eat, along with finding a toilet was necessary.

About half an hour later, the girls left the cafe to continue their drive.

"Oh no!" Arabella stopped in horror.

Safiyya stopped walking, looking at Arabella. "What?"

"We've got a flat tyre. I've never changed a tyre before," she looked hopefully at Safiyya, "Have you?"

Safiyya looked horrified. "No, I don't even know how to drive!"

Eliora laughed. Oh yes, as usual, the Lord's plans were working.

"But Safiyya. We have to take everything out so I can get to the spare wheel. Dad told me how to change a tyre, but I've never done it, and now my hands are going to get dirty, and we'll be late and miss the ferry." She chewed her lip, then shrugged. "I guess we just have to do it. Let's get the bags out of the back, and then I'll phone Dad so he can talk me through it."

Amidst piles of cases and bags, Arabella got the spare wheel out of the car, together with the toolkit her father had shown her.

"I know where to put the carjack. At least I can do that. I've seen Dad do it before," following her statement with grunts of disgust at having to kneel on the ground. "Oh my gosh, why don't people clean under their cars?" she said as her finger came out black from putting the jack in place.

"It's your car," Safiyya laughed.

"Okay, jack is in place. Do I unscrew the nuts now or after we jack the car up? I'm phoning Dad."

It took another thirty minutes for Joshua to talk Arabella through the process of changing the wheel, then they had to repack the car, by which time they were both dirty, thirsty and needing the bathroom again.

After an hour and a half delay, Arabella and Safiyya finally got back on the road.

Safiyya looked worried. "Just checking, what time do we have to be at the ferry? I know I asked, but I don't think we're going to make it. The flat tyre took up all our spare time. And, if we need to stop again, we will miss the ferry, Arabella!"

"I'll drive faster," Arabella said.

"No! Please don't drive too fast. That's not safe."

"But we'll miss the booking, and it's too expensive to catch another ferry," Arabella was frantically concerned. "Yeshua, we can't make it to the boat on time. Yeshua, please help us."

"Good," Eliora said, "Excellent."

"Remember your weapons, Bella," the Lord said.

My weapons, Arabella thought. "Oh! Yes. Safiyya, we are going to pray."

"Lord, we have to make it to the ferry before the last check-in. In the name of Yeshua, I ask you cause us to somehow arrive on time."

Time paused. The girls kept driving. The traffic grew heavier the closer they got to the city. Arabella looked concerned.

The girls kept driving.

In frustration, Arabella slapped the steering wheel and yelled, "In the name of Yeshua, I command this vehicle, with us in it, to be transported to the ferry in time."

Yeshua put His hand out and stopped the clock from ticking.

The girls kept driving.

"It's there!" Safiyya yelled, "I can see the ferry. Oh, I hope we haven't missed it."

Arabella looked at the clock on the dash.

"What?! How is that possible? Safiyya, look. Look at the time. Is the clock wrong? What does your phone say?"

"It's the same as the car clock. How did we make it? Arabella, how did we make it? And we have half an hour to spare! What happened? That's not possible."

Arabella laughed. She pulled the car into the ferry terminal and laughed. She laughed and laughed. "Oh, Safiyya, we have just experienced being transported by the Lord. There is no other way we could have made it. Yeshua, you are marvellous. Thank you. I asked you to help us, and you did. You promised Lord, and you never break your promises."

Arabella's heart accepted the glory contained in the words. They rolled around, swelling into a ball of fire and light bursting out of her mouth in praise and laughter.

The Angels in Heaven looked in wonder at the promise in this girl known as Arabella, and they remembered the words the Lord God had spoken before she left the Father's heart.

"The name your mother and father on the earth will give you will be Arabella. This name identifies who you are, your calling and your destiny. עארה Ara means lion, and so you shall be as a lion roaring into the realms above the earth, shattering bondages and chains. בל Bell, for your striking against the enemy, is as a hammer striking on an anvil, many, many, many, times. בלה Bella, for it means beautiful.

And so, you are." The Father paused and looked at the Son. "And 'A' is the first letter of the Hebraic and the English and Greek alphabets. A is for אלף *Aleph or Alpha. The first, the beginning. It is the first letter in my name of Adonai. Thus, you have my stamp of approval, my D.N.A. in your name."*

ACKNOWLEDGEMENTS

Special Thanks
to all those who participated in the fundraising for our charity
ONE SEED INITIATIVE
https://www.facebook.com/OneSeedInitiative

Left: India   Right: Kenya

Thanks to:
Michelle Palmer, Jenny Smith (Lauren), Bronnie Marlow, Diane Walker.

Your donations to One Seed Initiative meant the difference to a struggling Kenyan village in Kitale. I hope you like your characters and their interaction with Arabella.

The actual children's home that Arabella wanted to serve at:
http://www.thelifefoundationindia.org/

Maddison, my 14-year-old confidante, who gave such excellent insight to her encounters with the evil one and also with Yeshua: You are amazing. I am deeply grateful for your openness with these scenes. I wouldn't have been able to get this accurate without you.

As always, thank you to my pre-readers who stayed the course, encouraging me and sometimes pushing me along:
Tracy, Neomi, Paula, Diane, Jenny, and Brian.

Thanks to Steve Kioko for assistance with the wording in Chapter Thirty-two.

Thanks to Mike for his help with the New Zealand Police scene.

Janet! Mate! Thank you for all your work.

Colleen Kaluza: Editor, Publisher. Partner in crime. Equal mischief-maker. You are awesome.

And as always, thank you, darling Stan, for your strength, your shoulder, your safe arms, and your encouragement. Your sense of humour has sometimes irritated, but it is always needed. You are my strong tower, as well as a great washing machine, bed maker, vacuum cleaner, bathroom cleaner and all the rest of the things that I don't even look at when I'm writing. Always love you.

APPENDIX

All scriptures quoted in this section are taken from various versions/translations and used under the fair-use copyright law.

ארה בלה -Ara-bella

BELL – H6471 פַּעַם
stroke, beat, foot, step, anvil, occurrence
    1. foot, hoof-beat, footfall, footstep
    2. anvil
    3. occurrence, time, stroke, beat
        1. one time, once, twice, thrice, as time on time, at this repetition, this once, now at length, now...now, at one time...at another

CHAPTER SEVEN

Halberd – is a two-handed pole weapon.

Psalm 111:1 - 3
We give praise to the King
In the council of the upright
and in the assembly

The deeds of the King are great
Greatly desired by all who enjoy them
His work is full of majesty and splendour
and his righteousness continues forever

CHAPTER NINE

Luke 22:31–32
They thought back to another one whom the nameless one had tried to subvert. It hadn't been successful.

Ps.119.20 - 21
Be attentive to my words; incline your ear to my sayings.
Do not let them escape from your sight;
keep them within your heart.

CHAPTER ELEVEN

1 Timothy 4:12
Let no one despise you for your youth, but set the believers an example in speech, in conduct, in love, in faith, in purity.

Romans 6:2-4
We died to sin; how can we live in it any longer?
Or don't you know that all of us were baptized into Christ Jesus, were baptized into his death?
We were therefore buried with him through baptism into death that, just as Christ was raised from the dead through the glory of the Father, we too may live a new life.

Hebrews 12:2
Looking unto Jesus the author and finisher of our faith; who for the joy that was set before him endured the cross, despising the shame, and is set down at the right hand of the throne of God.

Galatians 3:28
There is no longer Jew or Gentile, slave or free, male and female. For you are all one in Christ Jesus.

CHAPTER TWELVE

Discordia - Roman Goddess of Discord
Trivia - Goddess of magic

Colossians 2:15
*He who had paraded them as a defeated army before all of Heaven.
And having disarmed the powers and authorities, he made a public spectacle of them, triumphing over them by the cross.*

2 Timothy 2:15
Do your best to present yourself to God as one approved, a worker who does not need to be ashamed and who correctly handles the word of truth.

1 John 1:9 *If we confess our sins, he is faithful and just to forgive us our sins, and to cleanse us from all unrighteousness.*

CHAPTER THIRTEEN

"This great mystery led to endless discussion amongst the Angels, as they sought to know the mysteries of God which were given only to man." Based on 1 Peter 1:12

CHAPTER FOURTEEN

"As Arabella drank in the written word of God, so Eliora also learned, for angels do not know everything. As Holy Spirit revealed more to Arabella, the angels looking on longed to know more." Based on 1 Peter 1:12

CHAPTER SIXTEEN

"That which you have meant for evil, the Lord God is turning to His glory and Arabella's good, to bring to pass, to save many people." Based on Genesis 50:20
Job 4:13
In thoughts from the visions of the night, when deep sleep falleth on men

CHAPTER TWENTY-TWO

"If you won't forgive others, then my Father won't be able to forgive you." Based on Mark 11:26

CHAPTER TWENTY-THREE
Mazzaroth.
Job 38:31 – 33; Exodus 12:1 – 4; 2 Kings 23:3 – 5; Psalm 147:4 – 5; Enoch Chapters 76 - 80

Further reading on the Mazzaroth: (accessed 29/10/2021)
http://eurofolkradio.com/2015/11/17/the-prophetic-mazzaroth-the-gospel-in-the-stars/

CHAPTER TWENTY-FOUR

The trees will clap their hands Isaiah 55:12
"Now that she is well grounded in love, the plans will be put into motion to teach her who she is, until she starts to understand the mysteries of Heaven." Based on Matthew 13:11

Acts 17:28
In Him we live and move and have our being

Matthew 28:18; Matthew 18:18; Luke 10:17
All authority has been given to me

CHAPTER TWENTY-FIVE

"Take your head off and put it under your arm. Look through the eyes of your heart."
Cheryl Davies http://www.heavensplace.org/

2 Corinthians 5:21
God made him who had no sin to be sin for us, so that in him we might become the righteousness of God.

1 Corinthians 2:16
For who hath known the mind of the Lord, that he may instruct him? But we have the mind of Christ.

Romans 3:3
For what if some did not believe? Shall their unbelief make the faith of God without effect?

Colossians 2:15
Why would I be afraid of a being that has lost the war? Jesus disarmed you, your rulers and authorities, He made a public display of you, having triumphed over you through His death and resurrection.

CHAPTER TWENTY-SIX

"Eliora gave her the answer. 'Even the stones would cry out...'" Luke 19:40
"'Even the stones would cry out...' She waited for a moment before saying, 'the mountains and hills will burst into song before you, and the all the trees of the fields will clap their hands.'" Isaiah 55:12

He smelled of oranges.
https://thequickenedword.com/rhema/OpenedSmellAromasList.htm
Psalm 114:6 *The hills gambol as little lambs.*

CHAPTER THIRTY

Isaiah 60:1
Arise, shine; for your light has come, And the glory of the LORD has risen upon you.

CHAPTER THIRTY-ONE

Matthew 18:19
Again, I say to you that if two of you agree on earth about anything that they may ask, it shall be done for them by my Father in heaven. For where two or three have gathered together in my name, there I am in their midst.

John 14:13 – 14
And whatsoever ye shall ask in my name, that will I do, that the Father may be glorified in the Son. If ye shall ask any thing in my name, I will do it.

1 Thessalonians 5:18
In everything give thanks, for this is the will of God in Christ Jesus concerning you.

"Yes, I can hold on to your faith, Jesus. Just like the woman who was sick for twelve years, held onto your robe and wouldn't let go." Luke 8:43 - 48

CHAPTER THIRTY-TWO

John 10:16
I have sheep in other pastures that you do not know of.

CHAPTER THIRTY-THREE

"To do this, my Father will be allowing the evil one certain access to her life." Read Job 1

Psalm 121:5,7
The Lord is my shade on my right hand. The Lord will preserve me from all evil.

"Be well and thrive, Arabella," Joy declared.
Isaiah 61:3; Hebrews 1:6; Galatians 5:22

CHAPTER THIRTY-FOUR

Acts 17:28
In Him we live and move and have our being

Matthew 28:18; Matthew 18:18; Luke 10:17
All authority has been given to me

John 17:23
I in them and You in Me— that they may be perfectly united, so that the world may know that You sent Me and have loved them just as You have loved Me.

Job 33:15
In a dream, in a vision of the night, when deep sleep fell.

ABOUT THE AUTHOR

Yeshua is the centre of all that Justine is. She is a revelatory prophetic writer, who is passionate to see the Church in her rightful place in Christ. With a lifetime of knowing the Lord, her inner strength and understanding of the things of God, shows in her daily interactions with others.

Justine and her husband, Stan, live in Auckland, New Zealand, together with their two crazy cats. They have two beautiful adult daughters.

Email: justineorme@justineormeauthor.com
Facebook : www.facebook.com/theauthorjustine
Instagram: www.instagram.com/justineorme

Have you read "In the Beginning - I Am Beryl" Book One (2018)? If not, it's a must-read!

This is the first book in the 5-book chronology taking you through the Biblical accounts from the perspective of the Beryl Stone, mentioned 8 times in the Bible, from before Time to John's Revelation of the end of time.

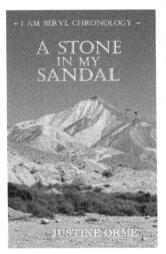

"A Stone in My Sandal – I Am Beryl" Book Two (2019) is the second book in the Chronology of Beryl. This time, we find Beryl among the Israelites in Egypt as he witnesses the transformation of Moses (Moshe) into a leader, and the miracles God performs to free the Israelites from slavery and then teach them who God is, once again. If you thought you knew the story of Moses and the 10 plagues, think again! Justine brings out truths many have overlooked in this historical and Biblical account. Don't miss it!

In "25 to Life" (2019), Justine writes with great power and sensitivity about the very personal and painful subject of child abuse.

Melissa's story is one of hope for all, which allows the reader to see that the only path to lasting freedom in any situation is through Jesus Christ and Him alone.

For 25 hours, we follow James and Melissa as they journey towards Time Weaver, and back to life.

"How Much is One Person Worth" (2021) Brian Taylor and Justine Orme.

How much are YOU worth?

Understanding how to set a value on your self-worth. Once you have an inner sense of great worth, you can develop far better relationships, and that is simply beautiful.

ISBN 978-0-473-60368-7

CPSIA information can be obtained
at www.ICGtesting.com
Printed in the USA
BVHW082004220522
637751BV00002B/43